I0822378

Teotl: In My Blood

Book 1

By Victoria Olvera

Table of Content

Chapter 1 : "Homecoming"..................... p.4

Chapter 2 : "Washing off a Memory"........ p.13

Chapter 3 : "The Tiger's Eye"................. p.30

Chapter 4 : "First Impression Money"....... p.56

Chapter 5: "A Sandwich of a Story" p.64

Chapter 6 : " Into the Woods".................. p.71

Chapter 7: "Show and Tell"..................... p.88

Chapter 8: "Love Letter" p.112

Chapter 9: " Diving in Deep".................. p.148

Chapter 10: "A Night to Remember" p.169

Chapter 11: "Mirror Mirror" ....p. 185

Chapter 12: "Wide Awake" p.212

Chapter 13: "The Wings"...................... p.219

Chapter 14: “The Truth” …………………… p. 240

Chapter15:“Rage is Red,Hearts are Blue”..p. 255

Chapter One

"Homecoming"

Numb. I felt numb after the burst of energy left my body. It was as if a flash bang had hit me and there was a prolonging ringing in my ear that lingered. I was very much struggling to catch my balance and the constant ringing in my ears was triggering a migraine-level headache. I guess I wasn't used to the Teotl. Maybe it was too strong for me.

It's happened before, to my Uncle Berto. He had an ability to hear thoughts at a global level. Sadly, it was too much for him; his eyes and ears bled out causing him to die in convulsion. It was as if a computer was overloaded with data and the motor had burned out. That's when my family realized the severity of the Teotl.

I struggled to get to my feet, and when I finally did, I found myself fumbling back to the ground. My head hung low from the exertion of energy that had been expelled from my body. The ringing in my ears gradually transitioned to screams. The confusion took over me, making me lift my head to look at my surroundings. At that moment, I saw the results of what I did. I didn't mean to do it. I had no control of the Teotl that was gifted to me. If you can call it that. Sometimes I feel that it was more of a curse than a gift.

I mustered up the strength to get to my feet again and struggled to walk over to the bent light post where Tim layed. His body was folded in half backwards. It looked as if his body tried to create a knot of his limbs around the post but couldn't. The screaming continued and I saw that it was coming from Gina.

Oh great, it had to be Gina, the town's biggest gossiper. I thought to myself and it dawned on me, "she saw the whole thing. Do I have enough energy to wipe her out too?".

Hehehe……Relax, I'm only kidding.
This is not a villain story…………..or is it?

Slowly backing away from what was now a crime scene, I stumbled and ran off to the one place I would be safe. The one place where they would help me find a solution. The one place I could think of was....home.

I couldn't help but think about the incident, especially how I was now connected to someone's death. My mind started to race as I thought about the severity of the situation. Had I touched Tim's body or anything else in the area? I began to replay the entire event in my head, as painful as it was to relive it. Luckily, I didn't touch Tim's body. I was relieved when I realized that I had not left my DNA at the crime scene.I don't think there's any way they can find out that I had any physical connection to the crime.

When I arrived home, I stopped for a minute to look at the front of my house. It really was a beautiful but humble house, with a large driveway and a perfectly manicured front lawn. The curved, cement walkway leads you from the sidewalk to the 3 front steps of the front porch. The porch gives way to the welcoming entrance of the home; a modest,six foot single oak brown wooden door with a fan window frame.

My mom stood at the door with my brother Georgio, who was sitting on the front steps. I couldn't help noticing a slight smile on his face. It's weird saying his full name. I normally call him by his nickname, Gio. Out of the seven of us, my brother and I have been the closest since we were little. We used to run around and pretend we had the Teotl and would kick imaginary bad guys ass's. He was the oldest of the two, so he was always the one with the cooler powers.

Those were the good old days when we were kids. Ever since his Senior year of High School, it feels like he has shut me out. It's been eight years since then. Now he's 25 and works at a library.

I continued walking towards the house. They looked at me as if they knew what happened. It was strange, the look on their faces was calm, as if nothing bad had occurred.

As I approached the house there was a strange feeling in the air, like it was buzzing. I wonder, am I the only one experiencing this? It seems only I can feel and hear this buzzing. Did I hurt my head in the incident with Tim? With every step I took towards my house, the buzzing got louder and louder and....LOUDER. I, once again, was confused and concerned for my life. Was I going to die? Is this how it feels before my brain explodes?

Gradually, the buzzing in my head began to fade. I now heard what seemed to be multiple voices that sounded the same. It was as if the voices were trickling in through a crack on a giant thick wall. It sounded as if the voices were murmuring at me. Eventually the voice became clear. It was Gio's voice.

I looked at my brother and his smile grew. I felt a warmth in my chest grow. I was just glad to see him actually smiling for once in a very long time.

In a split moment, Gio told me through my newly found telepathic connection, that he had taken care of the situation and there was no need to worry. I winced at the sudden information that was going back and forth in a matter of seconds. In all honesty, I couldn't help BUT to worry because the fact stood, I killed someone.

"What did you do, Gio?" I asked my brother telepathically. Hoping he hadn't stained his hands like mine.

I could hear multiple connections of conversations within his head trying to tell me everything at once. The conversations were overlapping each other, and it was almost difficult to understand them, or to know which one to focus on. But one of the conversations had more dominance and clearly said, “I didn’t kill her, I made her forget.” I felt a sense of relief knowing he didn't kill Gina, but it left me with more questions.

My mom and brother welcomed me inside. The three of us entered the house and went towards the kitchen. It has been two years now since I’ve been home. Not much had changed since I left. The old wooden table with the scratches on its legs still rested in the corner of the kitchen along with its nook seat. The curtains were, however, slightly different then they were when I left. They had a more modern look.

You’re probably wondering why I left. It wasn’t some rebellious stage or anything like that. I left because it was an academic endeavor. I chose to attend a college down south and graduated with my associates degree. Once I completed my degree, I decided to come back home.But as soon as I arrived, everything began to change. Things got crazy, it was as if my return home activated the Teotl. But I digress.

My brother and I sat down at the kitchen table while my mom stood by the sink. I began to tell them what I could remember. My memory was a bit hazy since it was so sudden. It wasn't that they didn't know what I had done, I was really telling them to help myself process what had occurred.

"The Teotl has gifted your life with its presence .Now it is time for you to learn to control it." My mom said as she began to make tea.

Concerned, I looked at both of them and responded, " What if I die?" I said anxiously, "What if I end up like Uncle Berto?"

Gio chuckled and verbally stated, "You'll be fine."

"Reina, calm down. It's time you go to The School of Tlamatini. There, they will teach you how to control your new abilities" my mother said as she turned to my brother and I with two mugs of milk tea.

"School?!" I said, baffled. " I just finished two years of schooling mom, I didn't plan on doing more years in another institution."

“Rei, it will be fine. You get to go to school where I work!” My brother responded enthusiastically while taking the mug from my mom.

“And you! Since when did you start talking to me!? ” I said slightly upset while taking the mug of tea my mom offered me.

“A few moments ago”,he said sassily.

“A FeW MoMeNtS aGo.” I said mockingly. “You know what I mean. I have so many questions. Why did you shut me out all these years and now decide we’re as good as when we were kids?”

My brother took a sip of his tea and said, “Well, first, you didn’t have the Teotl, and my gift arrived my senior year. If I even spoke to anyone who didn’t have a strong enough mind or didn’t have the Teotl, their minds literally would turn into pudding. I was scared that I would accidentally kill you. I wouldn’t be able to deal with that.” He ended his statement and took another sip of his tea.

“Why can I hear your thoughts in my head?” I asked slightly less upset. Now I was just curious.

"Oh that?! Apparently, since we were close when we were little, we developed a telepathic connection. Yours was just dormant until you got the Teotl. I've been trying to talk to you since senior year telepathically. But your head is so THICK ,nothing went through it," my brother said with a slight smile again.

"Oh fuck you! As if your head isn't as big as the billboard signs on the roads," I sassed back.

"aS iF yOuR hEaD iSn'T aS bIG aS tHe BiLlBoArD sIgN…" My brother mocked me.
My mom exhaled aggressively and said, " Ay ya dejen se de la jodienda! You guys are too big for this!"

If you had not noticed from this statement, my mom is Puerto Rican. She very much gives us tough love.

We both snickered into our mugs knowing damn well that we will never behave like adults if we are in the same room.

Chapter Two

"Washing off a Memory"

The next day, I woke up in my old room. How I got there, I am not certain. It must have been mama's sleeping tea. It's often good for relaxing the nerves and tension you may have. It normally knocks me out pretty quickly. I swiftly sat up. My headache still lingered but it was milder. However, it was nowhere near as bad as yesterday.

Oh man, I don't even want to think about the previous day. I can still hear Gina's scream when I recall the incident. I am not sure to what extent my brother went to make this incident go away. I don't want to know either. I sighed, as I brought my feet from the bed to the floor. I sat in silence for a moment and looked around.

The room still looked the same. The only thing that was different was that one half of my room was being used as a storage and the rest was surprisingly clean and dusted. As if someone constantly moved about my room enough that they would need it to be clean. There's only one person I could think of. And that person was the oldest of the seven of us, Evangelica.

My oldest sibling has a superiority complex. She thinks because she has super speed and uses her speed to create strong intense vibrations, that she gets the final say on everything. Truth be told, I've seen greater power than hers in our family.

I looked up to the door of my room and there she stood. A petite 5 foot, brown haired, pixie cut woman, with big brown eyes and a smirk that lets you know she was up to no good. She hadn't changed much from when I last saw her, except now she had a pixie haircut.

"What up Shorty?" I joked to annoy.

"Do not address me like that. You know my name. Show some respect to your superiors," she said as she entered my room and walked towards the windows, where small daisies grew in a red planter. It seems my room wasn't only a storage room, but also a greenhouse for her plants.

"Mkayyyy, I'm not dealing with your royal highness ass shit so early," I said as I got up to walk towards the door.

And just as I took a step in that direction, a sudden draft of air blew past me and from the window to a foot away from my face stood Evangelica, looking at me as if I was something that got stuck underneath her shoe.

"I heard someone 'awaken' yesterday?" She said presumptuous. "Whatever the Teotl gifted you, it's no match to me. So don't even think for a moment we're on the same level."

I inhaled to make a smart response starting with," Evan, you can..." . But with just those breaths, she zoomed out the door and was gone.

That's so like her to do. Say some dumb shit like that and leave. Just so she could be the one to have the last word.

I rolled my eyes to that entire encounter, then walked over to where my phone was charging. “10:45 am, damn it; For being so fast she sure wasted a lot of my time.” I thought aloud.

I had told Tobias I'd meet him at the town's square to catch up. Tobias was an old friend of mine from high school. We used to have a thing for each other back then but never acted on it. But that was then, now I just see him as a good friend.

I quickly jumped in the shower to wash off yesterday's memory. I know memories don’t work that way but it’s the best I could do. As I washed my body, I saw bruises that had appeared from the day before. As my hands passed over them, memories began to flash of yesterday’s incident.

Recalling what exactly happened wasn’t my favorite thing. I remember the morning dusk. Everything was wet as if it rained recently. The few people who were on the train with me promptly left the station after they got off. So it was just me. Or so I thought. Then I remembered Tim following me from the station when I arrived back in town. A little about Tim; he was a bit of an asshole and thought he deserved every woman's attention. He would make a great pair with Evan. I suppose since I wouldn't even give him the time of day, he became a bit obsessed with the fact. I guess you could say I was his forbidden fruit.

As the warm shower water continued to fall over my body, I recalled the entire incident and what he told me that may have triggered the Teotl.

"Come on Reina, who are you trying to kid? I know you want me." He said as he continued to follow me.

I continued to walk and quickly glanced back at him. "Tim, it's nice to see you and all but I am really just trying to get home." I wasn't trying to be mean but one of the things I really don't like is a cocky man.

I began to get a bad feeling that made me not want to be alone with him. Beginning to walk faster, I noticed his pace increasing also.

"Reina, baby girl. Don't be like that!" Tim's pace increased more.

Why did the station have to be almost three football fields away from my town? I'm just glad I shipped most of my things home. The only thing I had was a small book bag with a few items. I wouldn't have been able to keep my distance from Tim if I had to carry it all.

What a creep. How did he know I was going to be there at that exact moment? And what the fuck did he mean by "Don't be like that." As if we had some type of connection. Or if we had a thing.

"Tim, you need to STOP, just leave me alone and carry on with your day." I said in an assertive way as I took a quick take of where he was behind me.

I placed my hand in my pocket to feel for the pepper spray my mom had bought for me 6 years ago. I carried it with me everywhere I went, and today I was so glad I had it. Man, I hope it still works. At least enough for me to get away if I need to use it. I thought to myself as I continued to walk faster and faster.

Tim grabbed a hold of my bookbag, yanking me backwards. I fell on the floor, landing hard on the ground. My back hurt so much, I reacted in anger, " WHAT THE FUCK TIM! Why can't you take a hint!" I said struggling a little to sit up.

He laughed, " FINALLY! I got your attention.Who knew, that's all it takes."

I began to try to get up from the floor and he just pushed me back down and got on top of me, semi-pinning me down. At this point, I was scared for my life and my sanity. Mom used to tell the girls in our family to always be careful when walking alone and to always be aware of our surroundings. *Porque nadie nunca sabe. We could be raped or killed.*

The thought of it all ran through my head and made me want nothing more than for him to be as far away as possible from me. He began to try to touch me all over, in places I really didn't want to be touched. I began to feel severely unsettled and was completely appalled by him. The way he touched me made me feel disgusted and nauseous.

"What are you doing!?! Get off me,Tim!" As I struggled to get him off, I saw a blurred figure in the distance. I guess that's how Gina saw the whole thing.

All of a sudden my heart felt as if it was going to come out of my chest, and I started to feel everything around me. Everything that existed and its form and the manner it was created in, I felt. I can even feel each and every hair on Tims body standing.

Tim backed off for a second, “What the hell?! What kind of witchery?”

“I don’t feel well, leave me alone Tim!”, I said as I continued to try to push him off.

“Serves you right!” He said nonchalantly, struggling with me so that I would stay down.

And that was when all the energy I felt centered back into my body and expelled out as if it was a bomb that went off. The only difference, I think I was able to manipulate the force, leaving Tim to his gruesome demise. And the rest played out.

Shaking my head to forget about the incident, I finished showering and turned the water knob off. I got dressed and headed down stairs. Gio was already up and ready to go to work. He sat in the kitchen with his cafecito and a piece of bread. He normally is on time for everything. Even his birth was on time, not a minute too late or a minute too soon….or so I’m told.

“Hey. Where’s mom?”I said as I approached the fridge.

“Where she usually is. The Greenhouse,” he said as he took a bite of his bread.

I pulled the milk out the fridge and turned to walk over to the kitchen counter. I had taken a bowl from the cabinets above the counter and the clear plastic container that had the “Berries” cereal in it. That’s my favorite type of cereal.

After having a small breakfast, Gio left for work and I went to the back of the house in search of mom. As I walked to the backyard, I could see a 15ft by 10ft greenhouse with flowers growing wildly. There was greenery everywhere, as if it was a trapped jungle-beast, trying to get out.

The door to the greenhouse was open wide, naturally that ment someone was inside. I peeked into the greenhouse, finding my mom kneeling by some plants. I wanted to discuss what today’s plans were with her. She normally has an elaborate plan for the day.

“Hi mama!” I was happy to see her working on her Gardenias. Those flowers don’t normally grow with her but she is always determined to make stubborn things grow. Trust me, I know.

“Hey baby! Can you pass me the flower food that’s on that table.” She said as she slightly gestured a point wave with her hand towards the table.

I walked over to the table to grab the bag of flower food, noticing a piece of paper with "The School of Tlamatini" written on it with a date and time. May 28th, at 2:00pm. Naturally, I was curious.

"Uhhh, hey mom, what's this?" I said as I turned to face her with the flower food in one hand and the piece of paper in the other.

Too focused on her planting, she responded without looking at me," What's what, baby?" She said as she applied pressure to the dirt, compressing the seed within.

I took a few steps towards my mom to give her the flower food and showed her the paper. She leaned back to take a better look at it.

"Ah, yes. That's your entry day to Tlamatini." She said as she began to take off her gardening gloves.

I looked at her recalling the conversation in the kitchen we had from yesterday. "Awe mom, I don't want to go. They're going to make me study more, and ya estoy hasta la madre de estudiar!"

"Hey, hey,hey, hey, watch your language." She gestured to me to help her up as she began to get up from the kneeling position she was in. Without saying a word, she signaled towards the greenhouse entrance, as if to exit.

Exiting the greenhouse she said,"Listen baby, you need to go to this school. You have no choice. Otherwise more incidents like Tim will occur. You need to learn how to master your powers, and who better to teach you than the wise ones of the field? I mean, it is the literal translation after all, The School of the Wise", she ended.

"Here I thought I was going to come home and just relax over the summer, and just enjoy a calm non-eventful return." Thinking about it, I sighed into a pout while looking away into the distance. I swung my eyes back to my mom. She had an unimpressed smile on her face while looking at me as if she would personally drag me into that school if I did otherwise.

"Okay, Okay, I guess I'll go," I said, feeling volun-told, as we began to walk back to the house. "But what is the plan for today? I was going to go meet with Tobias but I think I might cancel, after yesterday and the energy sucking poltergeist in the house, I really just don't want to do too much for today," I said as I looked to fidget with the paper I still had in my hand.

My mom stopped walking and looked at me, "Poltergeist?" , she said, looking at me suspiciously.

"Yeah, she's about yay high. Pixie hair cut….", I smirked.

"Reina, don't be mean to your sister, I know you and Evan don't really get along but for the time being try too. At least for me." She began to walk again and entered the house.

"Huh? Mean? Have you heard the things she's told me?" I said following her through the hallway that led to the kitchen.

"I've spoken with her and she said she would try her best to behave. Now I have things to do today. Just some personal errands. You can stay here and get settled in better if you'd like," my mom said as she washed her hands in the kitchen sink and then dried them off with a nearby cloth.

“Sure.” I said as I pressed my lips together creating a slight smile, as I turned from her toward the kitchen entrance.

“Hey, Baby.” Mom said as she gently held my hand that was closest to her. “I know what you went through yesterday must have been traumatizing.” She looked at me furrowing her brows, expressing her concern. “If you want to talk about it……I'm here for you,” mom ended.

“Wait a minute, I haven't said what happened. Did you see it?” I asked, tilting my head quizzically.

Nodding with guilt in her expression, “ I had a vision . It showed me how it was going to play out , so I knew you would be ok.Otherwise, I would have sent your brother and sister over there.” She said softly as she let go of my hand.

Taking in the information I was just given, I had some mixed emotions. Thinking to myself, I did not get physically hurt ,no, but I did feel disgusted about the incident. It was a bit traumatizing, to be honest. I looked at her.

"Also, it was your trigger," She said as she prepared herself a small cup of coffee.

"My Trigger?" I asked.

"To activate your Teotl, we all have one. This one was meant to be yours. I'm sorry baby," she said empathetically as she finished making her coffee.

" Okay, so it had to happen," I said, now understanding that this was inevitable.

"Yes, but he was not supposed to die. That was unfortunately a shifted result from the vision I saw." She then drank her small cup of coffee and looked up at the clock on the wall. "Ahh, oh boy, got to get going with the errands. Things will be ok my love, just make sure to breathe," she said, taking the last few sips of her coffee and putting the mug in the sink.

"Alright, if you say so." I said as I turned to walk towards the stairs, and went up to go to my room.

"Also don't forget your entry day is in a few days!"She shouted from the kitchen. I stopped for a brief second to hear her out. Then I continued making my way up the stairs. I was not personally excited about my entry day but hey, what's the worst that could happen; I kill someone else, haha! I'm sorry. My dark humor gets the best of me sometimes.

"Tck Tck Tck" a tapping knock came from the front door. I stopped in my tracks on the 5th step of the stairs, wondering who was there. I sighed making my way back down the steps, "all this extra exercise this is making me do. Mom! Are you expecting anyone? The shipping guy maybe?" I began to head towards the door.

As I approached the door I felt this strong entity on the other side of the door, causing my pace to decrease. I stopped moving. I felt uneasy, I could feel the Teotl vibrating over my skin.

"Who is it?!" I said from where I stood.

Tck Tck Tck, again. They knocked again. Instead of verbally answering.

"Maaaaaa!" I yelled as I ran through the hallway and into the kitchen to where she was.

"What's wrong baby!?" She said, noticing the fear on my face.

"There's someone at the door." I said as I stood behind her like a scared little girl would.

"Ahhh, dummy, then go answer it." She told me as she turned to face me.

"YOU go answer it!" I said in a whisper shout.

My fear seemed to have begun to be slightly contagious, "You're stronger than I am Reina, I think you can handle it." She said, sounding a bit frightened as well and whispering back.

"WHAT THE FUCK IS THAT SUPPOSED TO MEAN!?" I responded in a shout whisper again.

"That means..." she said in a whisper....GO ANSWER THE DAMN DOOR!" Ending her statement in a clear shout. Her fear cleared out.

I scrunch my face at her as a sign of disapproval. I began to walk back into the hallway and in front of the door. I felt that buzzing in the air again, like the one I felt with Gio, but it was different. I began to hear a white noise instead.

Slowly reaching for the door knob, I took a deep breath. Quickly, grabbing hold of the handle ,"Fuck it!" I said as I opened the door aggressively.

There stood a 6 foot tall, black haired, chiseled jaw, hazel eyed man. He smirked looking down at me. The tension I carried in my body eased out.

"Oh, it's you."

Chapter Three

"The Tiger's Stone"

Unimpressed, I stepped aside to let him in. As he entered, I came to realize my siblings emanated sound, well at least that I could hear and feel. I wonder if they can hear it too? Or was it just me?

"What are you doing here? Also, can you hear those sounds that briefly show up and then dissipate?", I asked as I closed the door behind him.

He turned to me with a jokingly shocked face. "Well hello to you too, little sis. And yes, all of our siblings briefly emanate a sound only we can hear, Evan, Gio and I learned this after trying to play hide and seek one day when we were little," As he slightly shook his head in disappointment from my first question.

"Why do you look so shocked, Sebastian?!" I joked knowing well enough why he carried a disappointed energy.

Sebastian is my 2nd oldest sibling of the seven of us. He loves to have grand welcomings home and for people to be excited by his presence. He can be a bit vain occasionally but sometimes I think it's due to his compulsive ability that the Teotl gifted him. He was also gifted with extreme attractiveness. But I'm not sure if that was a gift from the Teotl or a gift from our parents.

He rolled his eyes and ignored my question.

"Mom! Your favorite child is home!" He yelled, smiling as he began to walk down the hall.

"You're not *the* favorite child." I said as I followed after him.

"Then how do you know I was talking about me?" He said with a quick glance and a smile, back at me.

Mom was beginning to prepare lunch. As we entered the kitchen, we could see her in an old faded red plaid apron with five embroidered flowers on the chest part of the apron. She looked towards our direction. She was grabbing some frozen chicken from the freezer.

"Ayyy!! Another one of my babies! It seems like everyone is showing up today." Mom shouted with joy as she put the frozen chicken on the counter and wiped her hands on an old kitchen cloth to embrace Sebastian.

I took a seat and started to fidget with the silverware that was on the table.

"Mmmmmm" she hummed as she hugged him tightly, rocking him with a motherly affection from side to side. The way she hugged him would make anyone believe that he is “the favorite child”. But if you knew my mom like we did, you'd know she hugs all of us like that.

"It's so good to see you Papito, how have you been?" She asked as she let him go to take a better look at him.

"I've been great, lots of traveling. The usual.”, he said nonchalantly, smiling. “ I brought you something." Sebastian said as he took a step back from the embrace with mom, to reach into his pocket.

Ever so gently he pulled something wrapped in a black silk handkerchief. He presented it to her as a gift.

"Ohhhh thank you!" She was thrilled to receive a gift from one of her children. Gifting mom anything was always a delight for us because mom always reacts as if it was the first gift she has ever received.

She looked down at the wrapped object and looked back up at him and squinted suspiciously. She asked, " is this what I think it is?"

He smiled ever so slightly, "I don't know, what do you think it is?" Sebastian looked towards the table making his way to take a seat with me, leaving the gift in her hands.

As mom unfolded the silk handkerchief a polished tiger eye stone began to appear. Attached to it was a leather string. It was a medallion Tiger Eye Stone necklace. Her eyes widened with excitement.

"It's beautiful! Thank you baby", she walked towards him and hugged him once more. He stood up to return the hug.

After her embrace she took a few steps back giving herself enough room to put the necklace on and to show her appreciation for the gift that Sebastian had given her.

It was just then, all so sudden, the ground began to gently tremble. I can feel the tremor beneath my butt. I thought maybe my rear was going numb or something from sitting too long so I decided to casually stand up. As I stood up I could feel the tremors becoming more aggressive beneath my feet. The table and chairs began shaking as well, along with the kitchen decorations that were on the wall.

The tremors were becoming so aggressive, things began to fall off the table and the kitchen counter. The kitchen cabinets began to open and close as if they had a mind of their own, the lights began to flicker as if we were losing power and regaining it a hundred times over. Could it have been an earthquake? My brother Sebastian and I looked at each other a bit scared not understanding what was going on. Or so I thought.

It couldn't have been any of our siblings, we would have felt their presence. Slowly we took our eyes from each other and slowly looked towards our mom. She blinked once and her eyes went from dark coffee brown to a pale white. Her hair was floating as if it were in a pool of water. But there wasn't any water at all, just air.

The house continued to shake, but my mom seemed unaffected by the tremors that were going on in the house. She was perfectly stable and standing straight unlike my brother and I. Everything around us seemed to be going crazy.

I looked at Sebastian again, "What the fuck is going on?!" I shouted.
Sebastian seemed to know but was shocked at the magnitude of what was happening.
"It's mom! Her Teotl is enhanced by a thousand with the stone!"
Mom began to slowly levitate in the air.

"Oh shit! WHAT THE FU.." , just before I could finish my sentence Sebastian snapped at me.

"Stop swearing so much! You swear like a sailor!" He said annoyed.

I responded equally annoyed, "WHAT? I didn't know she could fly!"

The windows began to vibrate from all the movement going on in the house. It sounded as if birds were pecking on the window glass a thousand times over.

Sebastian began to try to slowly walk towards mom without losing his balance from the tremors of the house.

“MOM! MOOOM! CAN YOU PLEASE STOP SHAKING THE HOUSE?!” He said, trying to reach for her.

Her pale white eyes blinked again and moved from a blank gaze to the both of us.
Sebastian quickly retracted his arm, uncertain of what she was going to do.
She began to yell in a different language,
“OCAMA! BOYA GUERICO! BARA BAJACUUU!
OCAMA! BOYA GUERICO! BARA BAJACUUU!
OCAMA! BOYA GUERICO! BARA BAJACUUU! ”

She yelled the same thing three times then slowly began to descend from the levitation. Her hair slowly went from floating to resting on her shoulders. The house began to calm, and everything stopped shaking. There was silverware and a few decorations that had fallen on the floor from the tremors. Some doors from the cabinets had remained open from what had happened.

Mom blinked once again, but this time her eyes went from pale white to her soft sweet coffee brown eyes.

She looked at us in a serious manner, and her tone of voice was as serious as well. She said, "We need to prepare and be united, something big is coming and it isn't good."

" Uhhh, I don't know what is coming but those blinks of yours, *son algo tremendo*." I said in spanglish still surprised at what she had done with her Teolt without trying. I can only imagine what she could do if she did try.

"Mom what were you saying, it seemed as if you were talking in another language." I began to pick up the silverware and Sebastian picked up the decorations that had fallen.

Mom helped also but then continued to finish making lunch.

"I believe it was our ancestral line trying to tell me something. Even though I don't speak their language, it was as if I could clearly understand

what they were trying to tell me. One thing for sure, something is coming." She ended.
I took a deep breath in, still trying to get used to the new "perks" in my life, if you could call it that.

"Oh-Kay, I'm going to get some air after that." I headed towards the hallway and to the entrance of the house. I opened the door to get some fresh air, and you would not believe what the view was. It was definitely not a pretty one.

I can see several cars had been flipped over with their doors open, and signs ripped from their poles as if a tornado had run through the area, touching everything but our house.

"What…the…Fu.." once again, before I could finish my sentence Sebastian interrupts walking towards the door entrance of the house telling me to stop cursing.

But as he approached my line of sight he yelled "WHAT THE FUCK??!"

"Bro…" I looked at him in disbelief, "Seriously, so much for telling me not to curse and you just full blown shout out a curse word? That's a bit hypocritical." I said annoyed.

He was so astounded by what he saw he ignored my comment. Before I knew it he had already dialed Georgio.

“Hey man, whats up…yeah… mom had done something by accident and we need your help with your mind wipe thing. Okay………..15 minutes? Sounds good. Alright see you soon.” Sébastien ended the call and looked at me with his charming nonchalant smile and said , “now we wait.”

As we waited for Georgio to arrive we decided to go back inside and close the door. As if it was all going to disappear and be good as new when we reopen the door. I, still trying to grasp a hold of what we just saw, vocalized, “Is no one else phased by the chaos that just happened outside? I know the Teotl can give people the ability to do supernatural things but this takes the cake. ” I shaked my head while still processing the extremity of everything that just happened.

“If you think that’s chaos, you should have seen when dad had that argument with mom before he left.” Sebastien said as he sat on the living room couch.

“What do you mean, I didn’t think dad had the Teotl?” I said as I followed to sit on the couch next to him.

“Well he definitely has it, why do you think we call it Teotl and not something else? Mom and Dad were both young when they met, he had his abilities before she did. So, they called it Teotl since she didn’t know what it was called and neither did her family at the time.” He began to say , “ do you remember that one day that we had a 6.0 magnitude earthquake?” Sebastien added as he leaned towards the arm rest to put his arm and brought his hand up to his face in a thoughtful gesture.

I sat back trying to recall the day he was talking about. “AHHHH yeah, I do remember.”

“Well that was dad. The only thing is that dad’s gift is from a different ....uh... group. Dad doesn’t like to use his Teotl because of that one day. We were all there but you were still little, so you probably don’t remember much. Anyway, we all were crying and scared of him for a while. He never wanted us to be afraid of him so he tries not to use it or at least get super angry. We have a lot of interesting stuff in our family.” He said as he crossed his legs so that his foot rested slightly over his knee.

“Yeah, I have noticed. Ever since I’ve arrived everything has been more intense than I last remembered with the Teotl.” I said while making myself more comfortable.

“Well little sis,that is because you didn’t have the Teotl before and the great responsibilities that come with having it. A little more on our father as you know, he is Mexican, and not Puerto Rican like our mother.” Sebastian continued to say.

“Yeah, so?” I responded.

“So his Teolt comes from a different set of ancestors than moms.” He said.

“Yeah , obviously,” I looked at him, seeing how he was sounding condescending.

Looking back at me and realizing it Sebastien went on and said, “Well, some say that his Teolt was gifted to him by the Aztec god Tlaloc. The god of rain, water , lightning and so forth. But some say that his Teolt could have also come from Tepēyōllōtl.” sebastien said as he checked his phone. He seemed disappointed from the lack of notifications he has.

“So what you’re telling me is that our abilities….they came from ancient god beings from our ancestral tribes?I thought it was just something we had in our family.” I looked at him a bit surprised.

“Mmhm, exactly. You will learn more about this once you start that school. What was it called again, the wise? ” He tucked his phone in his pocket.

“The school of Tlamatini” I corrected him.

“Same thing” he responded.

“Okay, so who is Tay-pah……..however you say the name?” I looked at him feeling more drawn to know more of the Teotl and the depth and history it had in our family.
“Tepēyōllōtl? He basically was the god of earthquakes, and echoes. And that was why many believed that dad was gifted by that deity.” He said as his face went from conversational expression to a serious thought. It was strange seeing how quickly a topic could change such a

handsome and charming face to a serious murderous one.

“What happened?” I said as I sat up straight from my comfortable position noticing the shift in his expression.

“She happened.” His facial expression softened.

I, still confused to who *She* was, I asked, “She? Who’s she? Bro…you’re vague as fuck.” I looked at him resting all my muscles from my face to show my annoyance. “I need more info my dude” I said as I leaned back in my seat.

Sebastiens eyes moved from staring into the abyss to looking at me with an old sadness that seemed to have been buried for years but had resurfaced.

“She…was AzaRayah.” Sebastien said as he began to rub a golden ring he had on his pinky finger, lost in thought.

I ,still annoyed by how long he is dragging the story, threw a couch pillow at him and said, “I'm going to punch you, who the hell is AzaRayah? Stop prolonging it.”

Snapping out of it, sebastien deeply exhaled, “It doesn’t matter anymore.... For goodness sake, where is Gio?” Sebastien said, snapping out of his daze directing our conversation to another point of topic, he stood up taking his phone out of his pocket once again to make a call, to then realize that Gio was calling him already.

“Yellow?” He answered. This was a way of us saying hello, and we’d normally answer a specific color. The only color we never said was black or sage, because in itself we had thought black was to mean that something terrible happened or someone died. Black was very drastic, Sage meant that we were in need of help or were in a dangerous situation. Evan taught it to each of us when we were kids, I guess we never grew out of it.

I can hear a bit of Gio’s muffled voice through the phone saying he took care of it , and he’ll be home soon. It wasn’t but 5 minutes I could feel the familiar buzzing in the air again.

“He’s here.” I said as I got up from the couch quickly to walk to the door. As I got closer to the door the buzzing seemed to get weaker. Opening the door I can see Gio sitting on the front steps looking out towards the disaster.

Feeble and pale, he looked back at me and said, “help” then he fainted.

“SEBASTIEN, MOM! COME HELP! THERE'S SOMETHING WRONG WITH GIO! “ I yelled frantically, because I couldn’t feel his presence. As if his entire energy shut down.

Mom came quickly from the kitchen, “Que paso! Why are you yelling like that!” She looked at the lumped over body on the front steps. “MY BABY!” She shouted and quickly went to him. She placed her hand on his forehead then chest. Looking at both Sebastien and I, she told us to help him inside.

“Bring him in quickly, I have to go make a remedy.” She quickly went into the kitchen once more. You could hear her frantic searching.

Sebastien had his arms crossed looking at me struggling.

“What the fuck man, help me out!” I said while trying to pull Gio through the front door and into the living room.
“You’re the one that can move things and stuff with your mind! Pick him up.” He said as he looked at me like I was dumb.

“I don’t know how to use it, I might hurt him.” I said continuing to pull Gio and struggle through the door.

“Ugh, you’re useless. Move! Let me do it.” He said walking toward the entrance of the door.

“Where are you going? Grab his legs!”Still holding the upper body part, I saw him walk out the door, inhale deeply and put his arms up as if he was being praised or something.

“It’s not fucking time for your vainess Sebastien!” I continued to try to pull Gio, but he felt heavier by the minute.

Suddenly, he felt lighter. I looked up and saw this tall, muscular man. He just picked Gio up, just as though he were a cake being relocated. I had let go to get out of the way and not hurt my brother while the man carried him the rest of the way into the living room.

“Where the hell did this dude come from?” I said, backing away. I cleared the area so that the man could move around and place Gio on the couch. After setting him gently on the couch the mysterious man walked over to Sebastien, who was standing by the door and looked at him with this admiration, I have never seen before.

Taking another deep breath in and out through his nose Sebastien looked at him. His eyes as he blinked went from hazel to a dark violet. It seemed as if within his eyes there was a violet silk moving around in an infinity movement.

Placing his hand on the large man's chest, Sebastien said, “Thank you for your efforts, please return as you were before this and forget about all of this nonsense. I release you, once you get home.”

The man walked out the door and disappeared. I still have no idea where he came from or how he came here in such great timing. But I am guessing it had to do with whatever it was that Sebastien did.

“I ReLeAsE yOu.” I mocked sebastien as I walked towards Gio on the couch.

“Mock me all you want, but you don’t know the half of it if I don’t say that. Some people become obsessed with me or bat shit crazy.” He said as he closed the door.

Mom came back from the kitchen and walked quickly to Gio. She had made something that looked like tea but smelled like something died.

"Oh....My...Gosh...What is that ? What did you kill?" I said covering my mouth and nose from the disgust I had of the odor.

"Ay pendeja, your feet probably smell worse than this tea," she said as she set the tea down on the small table at the end of the couch.

I, most likely in denial, said, "My feet don't stink!".

"I need you to talk to your brother with the mind connection you have." She said still looking at Gio but waving me over towards them.

"I wouldn't count on it mom. She couldn't even move him through the door. Let alone speak telepathically." Sebastien said as he sat on the other couch.

"Well his jaw is locked from all the mind wipe he had done in one sweep. It was too large of a parameter for him to do at once. I can't give him the remedy to help him heal at a rapid pace. So either you jump in now or he will die." She looked at me with this anger as if his death had already happened and she blamed me for it.

“Ok….Ok…I’ll try.” I walked towards Gio's body. I looked at her, very much afraid of my own power and what it could do that I don’t know of. Or even the thought of if I couldn’t use my power and save Gio in time.

I grabbed his right hand and placed my left on his chest where his heart should be. Maybe this will help, since it seemed to work with Sebatien and his goon.

I exhaled deeply through my mouth.
“Alright bro, don’t die on me.” As I finished my statement I felt as if my mind fused with his. I can hear and see all the chaos and people he had wiped since he got his Teotl. There was this one wipe that apparently was the most painful one. It was a set of parents. I can feel my body's eyes begin to tear up.

It seemed like a memory began to play out, of a young girl smiling in front of me. But I wasn’t myself, I was Gio. I think he says something to her, but I can’t hear exactly what he is saying. All I hear is a hum. The girl stared expressionless at him, her eyes, and ears began to bleed. Blood even came out of her mouth, it was like everything inside had exploded and the blood was leaking out.

I felt a great sorrow come upon me. But it was not my own.

Within a second, the memory disappeared into a smoke. Behind the smoke I can see Gio sitting on the floor almost as equally weak as his physical body.

“Gio!” I said as I began to make my way through this dream-like realm to him.
“Reina? What are you doing here?” He looked at me confused.

“I need you to open your mouth in the real world.” I said trying not to think of what I saw and stay on task with what was important.

“What do you mean?” He looked at me more confused.

“Just do it! Or you’ll die!” I said urgently.

“Okay OKay, jeez.” Gio began to focus and I can feel everything around me turning dark. Just as though the lights were being turned off one at a time.

“I’ll see you on the other side,” he said as he stood up the best he could and pushed my left shoulder into the real world and out of his mind.

I can feel myself waking up from what seemed like a dream or a trance. Letting go of his hand, I stepped back and looked around trying to make sure I was out of the mind fuse and back in our world. Gio had his mouth opened. As I looked around I stopped at Sebastian's face, he looked scared as if he saw a ghost.

“Well I guess you didn’t fall too far from the mama tree,”sebastien said as he looked at me holding a couch pillow for comfort.

“What do you mean?” I said as I sat down next to him.

“Your eyes….and you talked…. Like mom did in the kitchen earlier. But you didn’t float.” Sebastien said as he tilted his head in curiosity.

A large gasp came out of Gio's body. Mom was startled but pleased to see her remedy was working.

"What did you give him?" I said stealing Sebastiens couch pillow from him.

"Hey! I was using that!" Sebastien exclaimed, bothered.

"You *WAS* using it." I stuck my tongue out at him.

"Well if you two are done being childish, and are really interested in knowing what exactly I gave him....Let me know. Until then it's just an old family remedy." Mom said as she began to get up from the kneeling position she was in to care for Gio.

"Your brother needs rest now, so don't bother him. Today has been quite eventful and it's nearly time for dinner. So I guess I need to whip up the lunch and turn it into dinner food.

Mom always knew anything and everything when it came to food. Mom could cook a 4 course meal in a matter of 30 minutes. She was able to make any accidents and or errors in the meal look on purpose, and the dish would always taste delicious.

The meal was prepared and ready to go. I collected the silver wear to place on the mats on the table. Sebastien set the plates according to seat location. And the minute mom sat down it was like someone rang a bell to eat.

Evangelica arrived home."Mom! I'm home!" You can hear her hanging her things on the coat rack down the hallway. There was a sudden silence, then she zoomed through the door and flicked Sebastien's ear before sitting down at the table. As if she was a saint and never did it in the first place.

Sebastien and I were sitting at the table already with mom.

"Ow!" Sebastien reacted to the flick in a bit of pain and annoyance.
"Let's be nice to each other, it has been a VERY long day."Mom said as she began to serve the sides to everyone. Even on the empty seat where Gio's plate sat. I felt a bit sad he was down, and really wished he was able to join us.

"Gio.....Gio...." I tried to communicate with him telepathically, hoping I wouldn't push him too hard.

"*Dude, I'm trying to rest?...*" Gio responded.

I smiled softly , glad to know he was well. "*Mom made 'Linner',It's time to eat, come and join us.*" I responded telepathically while I began to serve the lemonade to everyone.

A few minutes past, I can hear heavy footsteps making their way through the hall coming towards the kitchen. Peaking in slowly we all can see Gio making his way into the kitchen holding his head with one hand.

"Smells good mom." Gio said as he sat down in his seat.
"What are you doing up? You're not supposed to be up. Reina, did you wake him up?" Mom said looking at me disapprovingly.

"I don't know?" I said while shrugging my shoulders and grabbing a bit of the buttered vegetables for myself. I couldn't help but have a slight smile on my face.

Gio took a bite of the food first. “MMMMMMmm, this is delicious mom.” Trying to change the conversation he took another bite and looked at everyone notioning us to eat.

Chapter Four

"First Impression Money"

The following day I spoke with Gio about the memory I saw in our mind fuse. He didn't want to talk about it much but one thing's for sure, he made it clear it was the first day he learned of his Teotl, and it unfortunately happened with someone he had really liked.

It was the day before I had to go BACK to school, The School of the Tlamatini (the wise). I wasn't really sure how to prepare since all of it sounded like some fantasy school. I picked up my satchel bag that was sitting on the floor next to the foot of my bed frame. It was big enough to fit my laptop, a notebook, 2 pens and pencils, and a water bottle.

"Welp, I think that's all I need to go to a school that's going to teach me how to control my powers." I chuckled at the thought of how crazy this all is and just the sound of it coming out of my mouth tickled me.

I put my bag down on my bed, now trying to plan out my attire. I walked over to my closet that was half filled with hangers that hanged no clothes,and five hangers that had an old hoodie of mine, two long sleeve shirts and a dress blouse, and a pair of pants . I had not been able to set up my things since I had returned so that meant I either had to go into town to do some quick shopping or wear what was hanging, because all of my things were not packed and sent in order. To be honest I sent my things quickly and left that place like a bat out of hell.

Mom had taught us to always make a good first impression, no matter the situation.

Checking to see if I had *First Impression Money* in my wallet, "And that answers that question." I said, a bit frustrated. I sat on the edge of my bed.

Hearing frustration in my voice Gio walked into my room.

“Everything ok?”

“Yeah…… just a little broke at the moment. I had spent most of my money sending my things home,and noticed a box is still missing and the rest of my things are out of order. Now I have to go to this dumb new fantasy school looking like a hobo.” I ended as I gestured toward the half empty closet.

“Or, here me out, you can start looking through your boxes you do have and put your things in order.” he said smiling sarcastically.

I sighed walking towards my closet, “That would be a good idea but the box that is missing has the majority of my clothes. I guess a note to self would be "get a job and track my box.”

“That's not a bad idea,” Gio said as he sat on my bed.
“But remember you did just get here a few days ago.”He stated while playing with a plush bear I had on my bed.

Pulling the hoodie and pair of pants out my closet, “This is it, for tomorrow.” I said as I turned to him with my arms displaying the outfit I deemed to be *Hobo style* .

"It is what it is."He smiled politely.

I exhaled, still frustrated. Then I began to think about the previous day and things that left me with questions and more questions. I decided to ask Geo about it since it seems he's been in the loop longer than I have.

"Sooooooo, I have a question…." I said as I put my arms down slowly while in thought.

"What's your question?" Geo asked, wondering.

"Well I have several questions but I guess I can start with….What happened to someone named AzaRayah?" I said as I joined the two hangers holding the outfit pieces.

"Well that's a name I have not heard in a very long time." Geo sat up straight as if I caught his attention fully.

"Well?" I bobbed my head forward notioning for him to spill the beans.

"Well...it was Sebastien's first and only love that I know of." He said nonchalantly.

"WHAT!? Sebastien? In love?" I said surprised walking towards my bed to sit down and hear the chismé. For those of you who don't know what chismé means....basically a good gossip.

"Yeah! Well she did die so I don't know how accurate this information is anymore." He said casually as he got up from my bed walking toward the door of my room.

"Hey where are you going? You can't just drop a bomb like that and just walk away." I said as I followed him out the room and into the hallway towards the staircase.

"How did she die? Sebastien had changed the conversation before I could find out!" I shouted down as he headed down the stairs.

He quickly looked back at me with a look that if it could speak it would have told me to *shut up because there's someone nearby.* I looked up to an opening door to my left and saw Sebastien coming out of his room. He looked as if he had just woken up.

"If you were that curious about it you could have just asked instead of shouting it to the whole house." He looked at me a bit grumpy from his slumber being interrupted.

"Oh heyyyyyy Bud-dyyyyyy", I said, a bit surprised he was still home. Last I could remember, he would always leave early to do his things, so it was a bit odd to see him still home.

He smiled sarcastically while scratching his head. He placed his hands in a downward prayer position and then parted them as a way to tell me to move out the way so he could head down stairs. I stepped aside letting him through. I then followed both my brothers down the stairs and we all went into the kitchen.I sat down on one of the seats at the kitchen table. Geo began to brew fresh coffee and Sebastien started looking through the fridge in search of something quick to eat.

"So! Can someone just spill the tea already, and TELL ME!" I said, unable to wait for the information anymore.

"You're so nosey Reina!" Sebastien snapped while hanging from the fridge door.

"Well what do you expect? It's juicy stuff" I responded while grabbing an apple from our fruit bowl that we normally have as our centerpiece of the table.

I did feel a little bad about what Sebastien said. I never considered myself nosey, at least not normally. Since I've returned, I feel like I've opened a new lens in my life. Yes, I knew of the abilities my family possessed and that maybe one day I would get mine, but I never thought of the Teotl branching way back into our roots and beliefs.

I bit into my apple, while looking at Sebastian and Gio, hoping they'd go on and tell me more about this *AzaRayah*. "Soooo?"

Gio, facing the counter where he stood finishing making his cup of coffee, turned around and gently shook his head. "Annnnnnd you're hopeless" he said as he pulled his mug towards him to take a sip.

Sebastien pulled some ham and cheese from the fridge and sighed. "Fine, I'll tell your nosey ass so you can stop bugging me about it." He took the bag of sliced bread that was already on the counter and opened it up.

While preparing what looked like a poorly made sandwich, Sebastien began to tell us the story behind his first and only love.

Chapter Five

"A Sandwich of a Story"

He applied a bit of mayonnaise on one of his slices of bread and then laid the mayonnaise side down on top of the rest of his sandwich. He turns around with his back leaning on the counter and holding the sandwich in hand. He says, “When I was 20 years old I fell in love with a beautiful woman.

She was breathtaking.” He then took a deep breath and sighed as if she was right in front of him and he could see her clear as day. Sebastien took a bite of his sandwich and continued, “she was just beautiful.” he began to describe her to us.

“Her hair was dark brown with the tightest curls. And her skin was the softest caramel skin. Her eyes..... dark as night. And her smile.....her smile can brighten up an entire room." He took another bite of his sandwich and I of my apple.

Gio got tired of standing by the counter so he sat at the table with me.

Sebastien, still leaning on the counter with his sandwich in hand, continues telling us about AzaRayah.

"We were together for two years, and we were very happy together. I was going to ask her to marry me." Sebastien moved to the table as well to take a seat.
"And then what happened?" I said taking yet another bite of my apple.

"Well I was talking with dad about it, I told him I was in love and she was the love of my life.He kept telling me that she wasn't the one and that I should have found someone else besides her. That 'love is something tricky, you should give it more time.' We got into it really badly and said some hurtful things. He kept saying I was still young and didn't know what I would be doing if I married her." Sebastien stops for a second to think.

“So I decided to leave with her and run away and we went to LA, but before I could even establish myself there and build a life with her an earthquake happened. And the ground began to open up, we were not ready for it, I tried to reach for her and she fell through the gap. It was a long way down.” Sebastien finishes his sandwich.

“ I’m so sorry, Sebastien, I really shouldn’t have pry.” I felt guilty and put my apple down.

“Don’t feel sorry, it wasn’t your fault. It was dads. He found out where I was and used his Teolt. He didn’t care about anyone. Not even me. But it’s over with. Dad and I have not spoken since.”Sebastien ended.

“Do you still love her ,man?” Gio asked and took a sip of his coffee. “Just curious.”

“uhhhhh, nahhhh bro. I .....", before Sebastien could finish, mom walked into the kitchen with grocery bags.

" Utede no tiene telefono? Aqui etoy, llame que llame, y nadie conteta!" Mom yelled at us in what we like to call the Puerto Rican spanish. She entered the kitchen very frustrated.

"There's more in the car, go help and get the rest." She said as she set her purse down on the counter.

We all squirried out the door to help bring the groceries in, as if we were going to put out a fire.

After we had helped bring the "*store*" of a grocery that mom bought, into the house. I went back upstairs to my room. Gio followed but was heading to his room. He turned around to look at me before entering his room.

"Hey, I noticed you only had a satchel ready for tomorrow." He said casually gesturing towards my room.

"Yeah! I think I should be good with what I put together." I responded.

" Well you might want to take a few hours worth of gear. That school isn't around the corner and easy to access. It's close to a day's hike through a large forest that changes every hour."

"Wait, what do you mean it changes every hour?" I responded confused.

"It's a way to protect the school and the people inside the school. That way no one can find it. The exception is the people who know the place and have been accepted into the school" He stated.

“Fantastic.” I smiled sarcastically.

“Just what I needed this week, a random ass hike in the woods.” I went into my room to reset everything I thought I needed and prepare for what I really needed, which apparently was hiking gear.

“Huhhhhhh” I sighed. “At least I was told in advance. My hobo close will suit just fine now I guess. Everything does seem to happen for a reason”, I thought to myself.

I pulled out my book bag I used for school before and stuffed it with a second outfit that I managed to put together. Some bandaids, *porque nunca falta el bobo que se corta.*

“Here’s some hand sanitizer, and ….. I need a pair of socks.” I said aloud in thought while gently tapping my lower lip with my index finger.

Beginning to head to find my mom, who now sat on the single person couch she had in her room, reading a book.

“Hey mama, I have a quick question,....” and before I could finish my question.

“ Yes you can “Borrow” a pair of socks. It’s in that shopping bag.” She said as she turned the page to her book.

I looked in the bag and found a brand new packet of socks. I pulled it out, and looked at her surprised.

“Oh baby, don’t look so surprised, you know your mama got you.” She said as she closed her book and headed out the room towards the bathroom.

“Also I had a vision yesterday about it, so make sure to take that brush that’s in there too.” She ended and closed the bathroom door behind her.

“She always surprises me.” I whispered to myself.

Walking back to my room I heard a mild screech but I couldn’t figure out where it was coming from. It faded away as quickly as it came. I couldn't help but feel it wasn't anything good. I began to think about mom's prediction the other day. What was coming, and how can we prepare for it? Could our ancestors not have been more clear with their message, or did it have to be so vague? I noticed that's a common thing around here. Is it just something our family does and I haven't noticed till recently? I have so many questions and no answers to them.

"Well maybe I'll get more clarity and understanding to these questions tomorrow." I thought to myself.

The day ended and everyone who was home turned in for the night. Since we had an early start the next day.

Chapter Six

"Into the Woods"

The day to go back to school finally arrived. I wasn't too happy about going back to do more studying, but I did have a bit of excitement about going to a school I've only heard of in stories as a child and through casual conversations my family members had while I was around.

We drove to a parking lot of a large forest preserve in the middle of nowhere. As I got out of the car I looked around and noticed a large field of wildflowers. Next to it was what seemed to be a field with hundreds of tall pine trees. We walked a good distance into the forest. I looked back to see how far we've come, and I couldn't even see the parking lot anymore.

"Hey guys, are we lost?" I asked, a bit concerned.

Gio, Sebastian and Mom were walking a few steps ahead of me.

"Nope" Gio responded.

"We're almost to the Gate." Sebastian added.

" Mom, I love you but did you have to come with us on my first day to this school?" I , a little embarrassed but somewhat happy I wasn't walking into this alone.

"Well, I just wanted to make sure you didn't kill someone on your first day." She said jokingly.

"I make no promises" I muttered under my breath.

"I'm sorry, what was that?" She responded sarcastically.

"I'm kidding!" I began to laugh.

"That's what I thought.... besides I have to speak to one of the instructors there about something important." She added and continued walking up ahead.

Looking around as we continued walking I noticed the trees were shifting. As if they were relocating themselves.

“Has it been an hour already?” Gio asked mom.

“Time flies when you’re having fun.” She responded as she handed out a stick with moss on it to everyone.

“What’s this for?” I couldn’t help but hold it as if it had a disease.

My mom turned back to look at me with a look of *God give me patience*.
“This is so we can enter without setting off the alarm of intruders. Now, no sea jibara and stop holding it like you’ve never held a stick before.”

I grasped the stick tightly as a form of rebelling. It wasn’t much of a rebellion. I had not noticed there was a slimy slug on my stick. When I grasped the stick, I accidentally squished it, causing me to drop the stick.

“Ewwwwwwwwww, it touched me!” I shouted in disgust.

My mom exhaled and rolled her eyes at me.

“Good, now pick it up again and let's go. You’re pendejeando mucho.” She said as she turned back around to continue walking.

It wasn’t much further when we came to what resembled an old sequoia tree, but larger. In my opinion, this was the biggest tree I’ve ever seen or heard of.

“Finally! I thought we’d never make it!” Sebastien shouted in glee. He quickly walked up to the tree and drew something with the stick that was given to him on it. The tree began to open from the roots up to a few feet above him. I tried to look past him but couldn’t see much of what was on the other side. As he walked in the tree closed up behind him.

“Wai..wai…wai..waaait ! What about us? How are we going to get in?” I said, confused.

Gio laughed, “Use your stick and draw a symbol from our roots. Like this” Gio took a pen out of his pocket and demonstrated on my hand a drawing of what seemed to be a frog with its eyes detached.

"I feel like I've seen this before, when we would visit grandma in Puerto Rico." I told him, still looking at my hand.

"This is the coqui symbol that comes from the indigenous tribe called the Tainos, it's a part of our roots. In order to open the Gate of roots you need to draw a symbol from your roots," he said as he wrote his own symbol on the tree.

"But half of us are mixed, how do we know which roots to *Draw* from?" I looked up back at him but he had already gone through.

"Well that's rude. He left me talking. Asshole" I muttered a little under my breath. I then looked at my mom for a potential answer.

"That's the beauty of being mixed, you land in more tribes than one. So you can pick any symbol of either tribe," she said as she drew her symbol and walked in leaving me as the last person to get through.

I felt as though I was put on the spot. I was overthinking which symbol to draw but the one that clearly came to mind was the Sun symbol. I had seen it often around the island when we would visit grandma. I drew the symbol and the gate opened up. I walked through and at first it was dark. At first sight, we were literally walking inside and through the thickness of the tree. At the end of it was a light that led to another outside space. As I approached it, I saw my mom, Gio and Sebastien standing there, waiting for me.

“Ah you made it! I thought you were going to be there forever.” Sebastien mocked.

I chose to ignore him. Up ahead was a beautiful, large campus. Behind the building of the campus was a large lake. A tad bit confused, I looked back at the tree we had just come out of. I walked around it and the surrounding area was very much different then what I saw a few minutes ago. I thought to myself, *did we go through a portal?*

"Something like that" Gio responded.

"Hey! I know we can hear each other's thoughts and all, but make sure you don't go wandering in without permission." I said as I walked back to where everyone stood.

"All right let's head down to the campus, you still have on-boarding to do and need to get your schedule and what not. " Mom interrupted and began walking towards the campus.

"All right, all right, let's get on with it then" I responded, still dreading having to do more studying.

Once we arrived there were many people there. All different ethnic groups. I mostly saw different Hispanic groups. And a few other groups that weren't Hispanic.

"So I noticed there is a large population of Hispanic people here." I mentioned as we walked into the office of the school.

Out of nowhere a 5ft man approaches us and says ," Actually our, school consist of 25% Hispanics/Latino/x, 25% Natives, and the other 50% is made up of many other ethnic groups such as a diverse group of Asians, Black/African American and some White/European American. We also have a few mixed students that land in more than one ethnic!." He ended while leading us into an individual office.

"This dude is short as can be." I thought and looked at Gio.
Gio smiled trying not to laugh.

He then looked past me, out the window that showed the hallway. He seemed distracted.

"I'll be back," he communicated telepathically. He looked at me, nodded and left.
Sebastien got bored shortly after and decided to go wander around. I'm not sure where or what he was going to do. In the end, it was just mom and I, as usual.

"Well that's very diverse I guess." I readdressing the man's comment on the different ethnics.I sat in one of the seats that stood in front of what seemed to be his desk.

My mom started walking to the entrance of the office we just entered and turned back to look where the man and I were. "Mr. Loyd, I know my daughter is in good hands with you. I really need to speak with Ms. Alma. If you need me, I'll be in her class."

"Okay, no problem. This should take no more than an hour." Mr. Loyd responded, looking at the both of us as he gently nodded.

"Great, all right baby, I'll see you in a little bit." Mom said as she looked at me with a worried urgency. She smiled at me, with an attempt to hide what she knew I saw on her face. And then she left on her way.

“And then there was one”, I muttered under my breath.

Mr.Loyd went through the process with me and got me signed in. He then took me on a tour to familiarize myself with the campus grounds.

He began to tell me the history of the school and how it came to be what it is today.
“ The School of Tlamatini was founded by a Taino descendant woman who went by the name of GiieGiie, which means Soul of a Tree. She had a son that was born with a gift that was similar to one of the Taino gods they had believed. Her name was Atabey, the god of fertility, she was also considered the earth spirit. Her son can make any plant sprout in a matter of seconds. She was astounded and worried at the same time. She knew if people were to find out, they would try to take her son and try to figure out what makes him tick. So she built this place for him. She later found out they weren’t the only ones and so she opened up the safe space to the other people. With time they realized that some of the kids sometimes didn’t know how to

control their powers, so they had the older kids guide them and teach them. And that was when the idea sparked. She turned the place into The School of Tlamatini, The school of the wise." He ended as though it were an *Aha* moment.

"So you guys will help me control my Teotl?" I asked.

"Yes, this is also something you will learn in class. Which will be starting in 10 minutes." He said as he handed me my schedule.

"Oh…okay…so this is happening." I said, a little nervous.
"Yes, all you need to do is head down this hall and then turn left at the last door." He signaled upward with his head, showing me the direction.

"Okay. Thank you." I took my schedule and headed down to the class. As I walked down the hall and looked around, I noticed the school had a college vibe to it. Out of nowhere, a puff of black smoke appeared and a tall muscular guy with short dirty blond hair had bumped into me.

"What the fuck!" I looked at him surprised at how he just pulled a reverse Houdini on me. Instead of disappearing he appeared in front of me.

"Ah! I'm so sorry!" He began to apologize. As he looked back at the end of the hall.

"Where did you come from?" I asked, waving the smoke out of my face.

He continued looking back as if he was worried of being caught doing something he wasn't supposed to be doing.

"Hey, are you ok?" I asked with somewhat of a suspicious but concerned expression. I took a step back to look at him better.

Damn this dude is Fine, with a capital Ffffff. I thought to myself.

"Yeah! I'm great, I have to go. " He hurried off. Clearly he had somewhere to be.

Still stunned by what happened, I continued walking to the class I was supposed to be at 5 minutes ago.

As I walked in the class to what looked like the teacher's desk, I looked at the classroom. The layout was definitely not in a traditional and authoritative set up. There were 15 desks max and the desks were set up in a large circle.

" Ms.Cuapa, there's someone at your desk." A student said letting the teacher know I was in the room.

The lady that was helping a student out with something on their paper, turned around to face me.

"Ah, yes, you must be Ms. DelaRosa." She smiled kindly as she approached me.

“I was told to come here.” I looked at my schedule and it had 3 classes on it. The first one says,

Class: Ancestral and Origins
Time: 12:30pm-1:30pm

“Perfect my name is Ms.Cuapa as you may have just heard from one of my students, please find a seat and join us.” She welcomed me to the seats in the class.

There were a few, so I chose the one that was closest to the door in case I have to run out of here. I still had all my gear that I was told I needed to get to this school, with me. I set it down next to me. I mainly observed the teacher and the class, which made me seem quiet and distant. I noticed everyone in the class I was in was roughly around my age. It's definitely like college all over again.

"All right everyone, we have a new member in our class. Make sure to make her feel welcomed after class today! Now going forward, can someone tell me what we just went over?" She looked at everyone.

A girl raised her hand to respond.

"Yes, Dina!" Ms.Cuapa called on a student.

"We just went over how all our abilities seem to branch off of our ancestors' beliefs. The gods that they once worshiped gifted what some of us call powers to their children and their children's children, and so forth. Also, that our powers originated from the abilities the Gods possess." Dina responded with the most annoying attitude I have ever seen an adult have.

"Excellent! That's right!. All of our ancestors believed in different deities and some may be similar to different ethnic groups but they are not the same. That also goes for how we call our abilities. Many call them powers, because it's the most common in our country, some call it Orka, some call it Orenda, some call it Teotl, and there are many other names for it. But it all depends on your origins and ancestors." Ms. Cuapa explained.

"So I call it Teolt...", Out of curiosity I decided to partake in the conversation.

"Yes, and that means that your ancestors come from the Aztec tribe. " She happily responded.

"But the Aztecs only reside in Mexico. What do Puerto Rico's indigenous people call it?" I asked genuinely curious.

"Unfortunately the Arawak language did somewhat fade away ,but modern day Puerto Ricans that continue the practices of the Taino people did decide not to call it something they possessed as a power but more of a spiritual essence, they called it Nacan. This word is pronounced náh-kān, which means balanced or centered, it's a place of power and strength. So when you have a gift you would initially have a spiritual essence of Nacan, which originates from the gods the Taino people believed in." Ms. Cuapa leaned back on an empty desk.

The topic of conversation was so interesting, I had not noticed the time flew by. Even Ms. Cuapa thought so.

" Oh boy, that's all the time we have left for today! Man time did fly by, huh?" She smiled and wrote what looked to be the assignment on the board.

" We actually get homework here?" I was bummed as I asked about it.

" Oh yes, but it's so we make sure you retain the information for future generations to come, when we are no longer here maybe you can pass on the information." She responded.

"No pressure there." I said sarcastically.

The class was dismissed and I picked up all the baggage I brought. It seemed pretty normal to everyone, I didn't even get side comments of how extra I may have looked. As I picked up my bag Dina, the girl with the bad attitude passed by and bumped into me causing me to drop my bag.

"Hey! You're excused!" I said, a bit bothered.

Looking back at me she responded, "Tsk, Obviously." She turned back around and walked out the classroom.

"What a bitch." I said as I began to pick up my bag again.

As I left the class, I looked at my schedule again to see what was next.

Class: Focal
Time: 2:30pm-4:00pm

" Focal? I wonder what that class is about?" I muttered to myself. I still had about an hour before my next class so I decided to just do the assignment we were given during the time I had.

I found a spot in a lobby. I sat on a very elaborate couch that was there. There were several seats and elaborate couches to sit on. Some of the seats were occupied with other students so I chose the seats closest to the indoor waterfall. There were a handful of people around those seats.

I pulled out a notebook, a pen and a binder to use as a hard surface to write on.
As I began to answer the prompt Ms.Cuapa had written on the board earlier, I could not help but feel I was being watched.

Trying to ignore it, I continued writing, but the feeling was getting stronger. I looked up from my paper to see where the sensation was coming from. As I looked around the lobby area, I stopped at a pair of deep intense hazel green eyes that were steady staring at me.

Chapter Seven

"Show and Tell"

The pair of hazel green eyes came along with a refined freckled nose. The jawline was so chiseled, anyone would think it could cut glass; and then, parted on the side, lustrous night black hair that went down to their neck. A seductive grin slowly appeared. It was yet another attractive guy. *Is this school filled with good looking people or something?* I thought to myself. Feeling flushed, I tried to refocus but found my gaze moving back to those intense eyes, but when I looked back he was gone. Somewhat disappointed, I continued writing. I felt someone blowing on my neck.

Startled, I frantically stood up and turned around dropping my binder and things on the ground. And there he was again. His arms crossed while he rested his head over the backrest of the seat that was back to back against the one I was sitting on. He smiled again in a playful manner.

"Uhm, excuse me! First, I don't appreciate your hot breath on my neck. Second, how did you get over here so fast?" I said as I began to pick up my binder and papers. It seems today is the day of dropping things cause damn, this is the second time already.

He got up from where he was and picked up my pen to return it to me.

"I like you, you're normal." He said as he returned my pen.

"I don't know how to take that, is that a compliment?" I asked confused as I took my pen from him. In doing so, I accidentally lightly stroked his index finger sending me into a split second of a lustful vision.

I quickly reacted and retrieved my hand. His hand still in the position it was when he was returning my pen, he looked at me sideways and chuckled.

“Are you ok?” He asked with a slight smile.

I, personally, was somewhat aroused by the vision and wanted to get out of there and throw some water on my face.

"I am absolutely fine and I need to be somewhere ....I mean I have somewhere to be." I lied, but began to grab my things.

"Ok, do you need help with all that gear?" He asked.
"No no no no, I am fine." I struggled to pick up my bag for some reason.
"Here, let me help you." He lifted my bag as if it was nothing, and set it comfortably on my back.

He then looked at me with a sparkle in his eye. "My name is Adonis, which is odd for most people since my gifts come from either Aphrodite or Eros. It's hard to tell sometimes." He began to tell me.

Then I remembered , Aphrodite was the goddess of sexual love and beauty. Eros was her son, and *that* apple didn't fall too far from that tree. He was the god of love.

"Well that makes sense. That vision took me off guard." I said as I began to try to walk away.

“Wait….what vision?” He asked as he followed.

“That one really spicy one with me ….and you…and a lot of …..Things going on, not for lack of better words.” I whispered, a little embarrassed to even say it out loud.

He looked shocked, and taken aback. “How are you able to do that?” He said, still surprised.

“Do what?” I looked at him confused as to what he was talking about.

“Well, I'm going to be direct with you. And I hope you don't get offended but, you went into what I call a deep desire but….. it was mine.” He said as he began to blush like a teenage girl.

What the fuck is up with this dude, I thought. Does he just go around thinking of people he sees, in their undergarments and getting jiggy with them?
“ I wasn’t trying too, I just touched your finger on accident and it just happened. Also, that's kind of creepy, do you do that often?” I asked, trying to pick up my pace to lose him, thinking about what he said; *a deep desire.*

"Well no, just to those I find attractive." He smiled as he followed.

He didn't get the hint, he was so surprised I *reversed uno* on him. He wanted to know more about me and my Teotl.

"Listen, you don't understand. I can draw out people's deepest desires, whether they are sexual or not, and even make people fall in love sometimes. But you like ...used it in reverse." He said as he slowed down.

" Well… I don't know what to tell you, my guy. I am new here, and really need to get to my next class." I said as I pretended to look at my schedule.

All of a sudden a girl yelled out.
" Doni!"

We both looked back at her. It was the Dina girl from class. She ran up to him and threw herself on him.

"So what are we doing tonight?" Completely ignoring me, she began to play with his hands and swung them as if they were a couple.

I tend to get uncomfortable in general when people over do it with public display of affection, so I decided to slowly back away from the scene and get the fuck out of there. But as I backed away I noticed Adonis's eyes never left me. I didn't understand why, he clearly has someone. Why was he so fixated on me? His eyes remained on me. Dina noticed it and it seemed like she didn't like it because she then grabbed his head and kissed him.

I laughed to myself.
"Territorial, much?" I reacted .

Adonis pushed her away, "what are you doing?" He asked her, a bit bothered.

I took this time to dash, and left that drama back there. Finally heading to my next class, I saw that guy from earlier going the same direction.

"Hey! Smoke Boy! " I hollered .

He turned around, and recognized me.

"Oh, hey. Sorry about earlier. I was in a hurry to be somewhere. " He began apologizing.

"It's ok, I've been having an off day myself." I said as we began to approach the next class.

As we approached the next class, we got to talking. While doing so, we felt a type of connection like we've known each other for a very long time, but we've never met before other than earlier today. It also turns out he's pretty new to the school too. His parents sent him here to get his *poofs* in check.

" So I just realized, I don't know your real name Smoke Boy." I said in a jokingly but serious manner.

" Oh my goodness, you're so right! I don't know your name either....well my name is Leif." He responded.

"Like the green things that fall from the trees?" I asked.

"Uh, not exactly. But it does sound similar." Leif said as we entered the class.

"So Leif, why do you have smoke abilities?" I asked as I chose a seat to sit down. He followed, sitting in a seat next to me.

"Well I don't just leave smoke, I teleport. In doing so, smoke appears when I leave and arrive. Unfortunately, I haven't mastered it. I one time ended up teleporting in the girls bathroom and well, let's say I had to switch schools." He smiled a bit embarrassed.

Before he could tell me what deity his abilities came from, a 6ft tall man with black short hair and intense blue eyes, and a charming smile interrupted.

"Welcome everyone, to Focal class! In this class, you will be learning how to focus your energy and power. You want to learn to do this in order to control it." The teacher explained. " But first I need to know what we're working with. Everyone please demonstrate just a small entity of your ability.

And the Show and Tell began.

He started from left to right. Everyone demonstrated as requested, some did well and some didn't go according to plan. When it came to Leif and I, the teacher looked at us, "alright, you are next."

"Ladies first", Leif jested.

“Uh Mr.Teacher, I don’t think this is a good idea.” I said, feeling the gaze of everyone on me.

“Professor Gregor is fine, Ms.....” The teacher said as he looked at me in search of my last name.

"DelaRosa."

"Ah, Reina. That means Queen in Spanish. Well your highness, you can stay after class and demonstrate if that makes you more comfortable." He said in a deep voice with a kind tone.

I felt bashful inside, causing me to timidly nod.

Leif looked at me with a wondering look on his face. I looked back at him and shrugged.

"Well I assume the best is always left for last." Leif stood up and looked at the professor with a mischievous smile on his face.

Poof, leaving a black and gray smoke where he stood he vanished into thin air.

Poof, reappearing by the teachers desk with more smoke appearing with him.

"Tadaaaaaaa" Leif said.

"Very good, Mr. Hansen. Now can you go back to your seat?" Professor Gregor said in a sarcastic and mocking way.

I picked up a small tension between the two, as if they had history between each other.

Rolling his eyes, Leif looked back at the table we were sitting at, and *Poof.*

Falling from above, Leif reappeared and landed on the table. His head was on the side of the table where I sat; he looked at me somewhat embarrassed. Everyone had laughed at the failure he had done in class.

"Hi." He said still laying on the table.

Looking at him with a pained expression, "I think you missed your seat by a lot."I joked.

He smiled and began to get up from the table and got back into his seat.

"Alright, seeing how that went, I have individual lesson plans to create for everyone. That being said, I'll be ending class early. Reina, please stay after class." Professor Gregor announced it to the class.

Everyone, thrilled to have an early dismissal, happily gathered their things and headed out the class. Before Leif left, he quickly scribbled on a ripped piece of paper giving me his number so we could keep in contact.

“Here, I’ll catch you around.” He said as he walked into one of his smokes, before disappearing.

Man, this dude has an interesting way of writing, I thought to myself before looking back at the professor.

I was somewhat concerned, not for me but for him. I don't know what will happen, once I start. The last time I used it unintentionally, I killed Tim.

"Don't worry, everything is going to be ok." The professor said as he walked to where I sat. " Can you tell me what happened last time you used it?" He asked to figure out how to help.

"Professor Gregor, the last time I used my Teolt.... I hurt someone severely." I responded recalling the incident that happened with Tim.

As I went into a trance of a memory, I began to feel everything around me again. The chairs and tables began to shake at first and then levitate.

"Ohhhhhhkay, let's relax. " Professor Gregor said, realizing what was going on around us. "It seems your abilities were triggered by a type of trauma." He continued. "I'm sorry that happened to you."

Snapping out of the trance, "Thank you for your sympathy. Do you think you could help me control it?" I asked.

Optimistically he said, "of course!"

I felt excited with hope. "Okay, thank you! " I said as I got up from my seat. "Am I free to go?" I asked .

"Absolutely! .....oh and before you go, just know you can always come to me if you need anything. Anything at all." He said looking down at me as he walked me out of the class.

" Thank you, Professor Gregor."
I said as I left the classroom entrance.

"One last class", I said as I pulled out my schedule I had shoved in my pocket.

Class: History
Time: 4:10:pm-5:10pm

We were let out 45 minutes early, so I had to figure out what to do with the time I had free. My stomach began to rumble.

*I think it's about that time, lunch time,*I thought to myself. Wondering if they had a cafeteria or place to eat, I began to walk around looking for something related to food. I then decided to shoot Leif a text.

Hey it's Reina! Anything good to eat around here? I can't seem to find the cafeteria.

He took what felt like forever to respond. I think it was because I was so hungry.

When he finally responded I had found a vending machine.

"Hmmmm….. what do I want?" I thought out loud.

Just while I was looking at the snacks and chips they had, I heard a harmonious humming. It had a similar buzzing sound to it like with Gio, except it was a little out of tune, like it was missing something. Out of the corner of my eye I could see two silhouettes approaching me.

I quickly reacted in a karate pose I created at the moment. Seeing who it was, I put my defenses down and yelled happily, "Heyyyyyyyyy!!"

It was the triplets, minus one. My younger siblings, excited to see me, approached me with arms wide open.

"Reina!! You're finally back!" Lyla said.

"Lumiere, Lyla! You guys look so big! Was I gone that long? Where's the third musketeer?" I joked. The glee in their faces slowly faded away.

"What's wrong?" I asked, feeling a concerned energy in the air. Lyla is hesitant to say.

"We can't find Liriden", Lumiere blurted out.

"What do you mean you can't find him?" I asked, feeling confused by the thought of them losing an entire person. Especially since they are constantly together.

The triplets were born on the 3rd day of the 3rd month at the 3rd hour. It was commonly seen for the triplets to do things in threes. Whether that was visiting on dates that add up to multiples of three's, or three times a week. Sometimes it was specific hours like 3 pm, and for shits and giggles they would visit at 3 am. Which mom wasn't fond of since it interrupted her sleep. They've been doing a lot on campus so they stay there in a dorm with the room number, 333. Mom had told me about this once when I was back at the other college I had recently returned from.

Unlike me, a late bloomer in this world, they received their Teotl when they were 9. They're now 17, goofy, mischievous, and always up to something. The gift that equally took something from them as much as it gave, was the gift of prophecies, but it only seems to happen when they are all together holding hands. They also were able to develop individual abilities.

Lumier had the gift to create light so bright it was blinding, sometimes it would create heat and could burn things. Liriden was more of an earth crafter, he can make plant life grow anywhere. Even plants that are not native to certain areas. When he was 10, he wanted to eat a mango but it was out of season, so he decided to grow a mango tree. It grew in a matter of seconds and died shortly after he plucked the amount he wanted. Lyla, on the other hand, was given the ability to control water. Which sucked when it came to showers in a house of 8 people and demanded it to be her turn. I began to think of what they said.

"So is Liriden 'missing' missing or is he just missing like you have not seen him in a few hours?" I asked, refocusing on the situation at hand.

"More like a few days." Lumiere responded.

"HE'S BEEN MISSING FOR FEW DAYS?" I yelled, surprised and a bit upset that they are just now bringing this to my attention.

"Wait...can't you guys communicate like Gio and I? And find him like that?", I asked.

"No...we don't have telepathic communication." Lumiere said.

"Yeah we are only able to see the future and prophecies together." Lyla added.

"Oh ok....Did you tell anyone else about this? Like I don't know, mom for example?" I snapped frustratedly after the fact.

Worried, Lyla said, "Well we didn't want to get in trouble so we've been trying to find him on our own."

Cupping my hands, and bringing them to my face feeling a bit stressed, I reassured them that everything was going to be okay but this was something we absolutely needed to tell mom. Having this on my mind, I couldn't even go to the third class. You see, when the triplets received their Teolt they became differently abled all together. They got what I call the "partials". Lyla became partially blind and needed glasses. Lumier is partially deaf so he needs his hearing aids. And Liriden is mute, well partially. The doctors call it Selective Mutism. That's when you can't speak in certain spaces but you may be able to in others. The space he tends to speak more is at home.

Since the triplets are so close to each other, they developed something similar to Gio and I. You can often see them looking at each other as if something is being said between them but you just can't hear it, only they can. There is one small difference, they also can feel each other's pain. Which was something I thought about.

"Well he's not hurt, so that's a good thing." I said as I began to walk towards a cross section of a hall.

I began to text mom.

Hey Mom, where are you?

I am in room 217, are you done with classes?

Not quite, we have a problem, on my way.

We headed to the room mom was in. As we entered you can see her working on something with that lady she mentioned from earlier. I think her name was Ms.Alma. Whatever they were working on seemed serious. There were piles of papers and they were moving papers back and forth on a table.

"It's another dead end." Mom said to the lady.

"What about this one?" Ms.Alma responded as she gave her one of the sheets of paper that they were looking through.

"Oh, hey babies!" Mom said thrilled to see all of us.

"Hi mom!" Lumiere and Lyla said synchronically.

Walking up to her with a bit more pace in my step.
"Mom, we have a problem." I said trying to keep my cool.

Looking at me with sadness, she said, " I know, I've been trying to figure out a solution but I can't seem to find it."

"So you know, Liriden's missing?" I asked, not entirely surprised.

"He's not missing Reina. He's been kidnapped." She said continuing to rummage through more of the papers with Ms.Alma

Lumiere and Lyla looked at each other concerned.

"And you think the answer is in these papers?" I said as I picked one up. It seemed to have a different and old dialect written on it. Lifting the sheet up, I looked at mom and back at the paper. "Mom, do you know how to read this?"

"Not really, I've just seen something similar in one of my visions earlier so I thought it would be a good place to start." Mom responded.

Lumiere and Lyla approached the table more. With both heads tilted they both said, "We can read it."
"Of course you can, is there anything else you guys can do?" I said sarcastically, joking.

"I can move my finger like this." Lumiere demonstrated his double jointed thumb.
Lyla gasped, "Me too!"

Then they were both demonstrating their double jointed thumbs.

"Oooookay, let's focus. Liriden, still missing. What does this say?" I asked.

“ Well this one is about herbs and medication.” Lyla said.
“This one is.... a poem?.” Lumiere said, putting his lips into a pout.

“ Through the eyes
With despise,
Lies
A heart cold as ice
Dark skies
Nothing flies,
Whilst everything dies,
It ends here,
Just you and I” Lumiere ended.

“Well that’s fucking depressing.” He said.

“Yeah and ominous.”Lyla added.

“Does that sound like what you saw?” Ms. Alma said, slowly standing up from her seat.

“Yes, exactly like what I saw. Just before....” Mom was interrupted by Lumiere and Lyla’s sudden scream of agony. Falling to the floor, “ MOM! IT HURTS! SOMETHING IS HURTING HIM!” they shouted as they held onto their legs.

"Let me see!" Ms.Alma said as she quickly got down to where they were on the floor.

As they lifted their pants from the bottom, you can see these marks begin to show. It was like they had been whipped with something and beaten from the waist down. All over their legs, you could see what looked like black veins. Ms. Alma was shocked and quickly grabbed both Lyla and Lumieres legs. Ms. Alma was apparently a healer of some sort. She began to heal them as much as she could before she passed out.They were too much for one healer to heal. I quickly caught her before she had fallen over. Mom told me to sit her on a chair while Ms. Alma regained consciousness.

After about 30 minutes Ms. Alma was awake again and very dehydrated as if she had run a 50k marathon. Lyla and Lumiere had been healed enough that they could stand back up. But they still had some of the markings lingering. Mom said this was just the beginning. Mom created a special tea for Lyla and Lumiere to help with the ongoing pain. We are hoping that we can solve the pains once we find Liriden.

Chapter Eight

"Love Letter"

It was hard for me because mom wanted me to focus on learning what I needed to know in order to control my power. But my thoughts were never in the class, they were always elsewhere thinking about who would have such a motive to kidnap Liriden. It's not like he could have offended anyone, he can't even talk outside of home. It's been 2 days since the incident with Lyla and Lumiere.

It was also the last time since I have seen Leif. Sebastien has been going around both on campus and around home, trying to help and see if he can persuade anyone to speak on anything they may have seen. The only things he had gotten were roses, some obsessive love letters and a coupon that said "One free lick" with a kissed lipstick stain on it.

"These people are despicable." Sebastien said with an unimpressed face but still flattered by all he's received in the search of Liriden.

"Oh get over yourself Sebastien, remember it's not about you. We're looking for Liriden." I said as I grabbed one of the bags he had filled with love letters.

"Jesus! How many did you get?" I exclaimed.

"I don't know, a little over one hundred." He said casually.
"Any luck." I said as I pulled a letter out of the bag.
"No", he responded with a sad and disappointed tone.

One thing about us is that we may be different in character and personality, and sometimes we just don't like each other, but we always stick together in the end. We feel each other's joys and sorrows. Of course, not as intense and deep like the triplets, but in a very united way. But right now, we are all feeling defeated because there's nothing we can do.

I looked at the letter at hand, it was from someone named Stephanie Munoz.

“Stephanie? Isn’t that the girl that Gio’s talking to?” I said first looking at the letter and then at Sebastien.

“ Hey, I didn’t even touch the girl. All I did was talk to her, released her and left. The next thing I know, I found that letter in my satchel.” He said.

I decided to open the letter. As I read the letter, I could feel the temperature in my body rising from feeling upset.

“ That bitch.” I said, shoving the letter into the bag. “Did you read her letter?” I asked, pissed off.

“No, I haven’t had the chance to.” He said nonchalantly.

“Well she’s a hoe, and we have to tell Gio about it.” I said, still agitated from the letter.
“She could have been influenced by my Teotl, don’t be so hard on her.” He said, looking at me as if he wanted to tell me to relax.

“Well according to that letter, she says otherwise.” I said giving him the bag back.

“Why are you so upset? He said taking the bag back.

“Because she's playing with one of my brothers' hearts and I don’t like that. She can go play with her own heart if she wants, but leave my brothers alone.” I said walking away. I wasn’t sure where I was going but I just needed to be somewhere else to cool off.

The audacity of that bitch. And to bluntly say that. Does she have no scruples or morals? Ooohhhh, when I see her I am going to give her a piece of my mind.

As I was on campus again, I found myself in an empty classroom. With one other person sitting with his feet up on the table, he had headphones on. It was Adonis.

Great, just what I needed. This maniac again. I thought to myself. *Maybe he didn’t see me*. I began to slowly back out. And just before I could walk out the door frame, he called out to me.

“Hey! …..I am so glad to see you again.” He said, as he quickly got up and walked towards me.

"Ah-ha-ha -heyyyyy" I said, slowly forcing a smile on my face. I turned to him trying to think of many ways to get away again. There's something about this dude that unsettles me. I don't know what it is. Maybe it was that incident from a few days ago.

"I never got your name." He said with hopes in his eyes to get it.

"Um, Reina." I said looking back to face him.

He smiled with that charm spilling out of his teeth. "Oh, *Mi Reina*." He said looking into my eyes.
I couldn't help but blush a little.

However, I quickly snapped out of it. I heard Gio's voice out in the hall talking to a female voice. And it was then, I recognized that annoying voice. I made my way out the door; Adonis followed me for some reason.

"Oh, hey Reina!" Gio said, looking past the girl to see me.
"Hey Gio." I said in a stern voice. The girl turned around to look at me.

"Oh hey Reina." She said casually.

"Oh please" I said disgusted by the sight of her.

"Well clearly you remember my sister, Stephanie." Gio said, looking at me as if there was something wrong with me.

"Well yes, how can I forget." She smiled and gave me a playful nudge.
"Drop dead." I responded and walked away.

I can feel Gio trying to get in and communicate telepathically but I was so bothered by her I pushed him out.

At this point I just wanted to go home. If it wasn't a fucking journey I would have left already. Still following me was Adonis. I stopped abruptly, causing him to bump into me. I turned around.

"What do you want dude?" I said in the straightest face I could make.
"I ....just noticed you were upset and wanted to make sure you were ok." He said taking a step back from me.

"Why? Why do you care? Don't you have someone to go to like, I don't know ....Dina, maybe?" I asked.

He scuffed, “Dina? We hooked up once and I tapped into her desires, something I greatly regret. Now I can’t get her to leave me alone.”

“Pue, ¿quién te manda a jugar con la gente?” I asked.

“I don’t know what that means.” He responded.

“It means, Who told you to play with people?” I couldn’t help looking at him as if he was a numbnut.

“I mean, she was there and I am who I am.” He looked at me as if he wanted to partly take back what he just said.

I smiled at him as if he gave himself away, “That’s fucked up, but I am only going to tell you this once. If you don’t stop bothering me, we will have problems.”
“If it gives me your attention then I’ll make chaos in your presence.” He said, smiling down at me.
Now I was the one scuffing, “I don’t have time for this.” I walked away. Thankfully he didn’t follow.

The following day was the weekend so I went home. Mom wanted all of us home this weekend. It seems Liriden missing made her want all her chickitties in the nest. It was pouring rain outside and some thunder here and there. I walked to the kitchen from the living room where I was sitting on the couch with my feet up,looking out the window. Before entering, I could hear the clancking of a spoon in a coffee cup. As I walked in, Gio was there with his daily cafecito.

He looked up at me, "Hey".

"Hey". I said going to the kitchen cabinet to look for some cereal.
"So what was that about, yesterday?" He asked, taking a sip.
"Look , I'm sorry, but Stephanie's a .." I didn't finish it out loud but I thought it loud enough that Gio could clearly hear it.
"Why do you think that about her? She's the sweetest girl I have ever met. We've been talking for a while, she has nothing but nice things to say about you." He obviously was defending her.
"Ay, por favor. That bitch can go drown, with her egocentric ass self." I said pulling a box of cereal out the cabinet.
"I don't appreciate you talking about her like that. She's my girlfriend." He admitted.

"HaHahahaHA stoooooop." I said sarcastically.
"I'm serious. We've been dating for two weeks now. " He stated.
"First of all, I can't believe that for someone who has the abilities you have and the tele-pathical connection we have, you can't see or think clearly. You let a woman cloud your judgment." I responded as I grabbed a bowl out of another cabinet.

"That's not true," He said, clearly bothered.
"Your judgment is so clouded you can't even see the letter I am trying to show you right now." I said as I thought hard about the letter so he could see.

In denial and not wanting to acknowledge it, he angrily got up and left the kitchen, leaving his cup on the table.

"¡Aquí no hay sirvienta!" I shouted at the entrance of the kitchen in hope he heard it down the hall.

As I began to pour the cereal and then milk, an ominous feeling came upon me. I felt I was being watched, why is it that this has become a common feeling nowadays. It gave a chill that ran through my spine. I stopped pouring the milk and looked around the kitchen and stopped at the kitchen window. And just faintly I saw a dark hooded figure in the distance. Standing under the rain by a tree.

I knew better than to go out there by myself. I've seen plenty of movies where the dumb chick goes out and then gets killed or taken. I don't think so.
"Mom!" I yelled, still staring at the figure.
"Yes!" She responded from her room upstairs.

Lumiere walked in with Evangelica talking about something.
"Why are you standing like that, and why do you look like you've seen a ghost?" Evangelica sassed. Lumiere sat down to grab a centerpiece fruit from the table.
I glanced at both of them and turned back to look at the figure, but it was gone.

" There's someone out……side" I said, confused by the fact that they were gone.

Walking to the kitchen window, "I don't see anyone." Lumiere said as he bit into a pear.

"Lumiere, have you and Lyla had any of the pains from Liriden recently?" I asked.

Taking another bite he turned to me, "no, but we're still looking for him."

"I feel like our family is being attacked or something." I said to both of them.

"Are you sure you're not making things up for attention? " Evangelica said.

I rolled my eyes at her. "No, there was definitely someone there." I said, bothered by her comment.

A banging from the door began.

BANG! BANG! BANG!

All of us jumped from the scare. We walked out into the hallway.
"Evan, go open the door." I said to her.
"As if, you go open it." She responded.
"I'll go open it." Lumiere said as he walked between the both of us.

"I don't think so." Evan and I both said pulling him back from both shoulders.

“I’m a man, I can protect you guys.” He said as he stepped backwards from our pull.

BANG! BANG! BANG!

Again, the door went.
“We’re older so we need to protect you” I said looking at him.
“Exactly.” Evan agreed.

That was probably the first and last time we will ever agree on something.

BANG! BANG!

“Who the fuck is at the door!?” Sebastien shouted as he came down the stairs from his room. “And couldn’t any one of you answer it.” He said looking at us, that now stood in the hall.

Unlocking the door, looking back at us shaking his head, he opened the door. Turning around to see who it was, he took a step back with a shocked look on his face.

“It’s impossible.” He said. “You….” he continued.

“Hi Sebastien. Can I come in?” a woman's voice said.

Letting the woman pass, you can see she was wearing a black poncho with muddy rain boots.

“I saw you….” Sebastien continued, looking a bit distraught from the presence of the women.
“Sebastien, who’s this lady? I asked.

“AzaRayah.” Gio said as he began to descend from the stairs.

Sebastien gulps, and then sighs, “ I saw you die. I mourned you.” He told her.
“Well you saw me fall. You assumed I died.” She responded.
“It’s been so many years, why ….? What are you…? I feel confused.” Sebastien said as he closed the door to sit down on the living room couch.
“I’m sorry, maybe I should not have come.” AzaRayah said as she attempted to scurry out.
“No! Don’t go!” Sebastien said, reaching out for her hand snapping back into the reality that now stood in front of him.
“I just needed a second. Please don’t go. We need …to …talk.” He said slowly reaching for her hands to embrace.

There was something off about this but lately there's been a lot going on so, maybe I'm just suspecting anyone of something bad.

Sebastien and AzaRayah were able to spend some time together and catch up the past few days. She apparently survived the incident that happened many years ago and was in recovery for half the time. It wasn't until recently she was able to come to him, Or so she says.

Sebastien was so occupied with the presence of her that he left the mission of the bag of letters for the rest of us to continue reading in order to find some type of clue to where Liriden was. Unfortunately, there was a lot of lovey dovey stuff. Some crazy and just one that was interesting. We continued our research at Tlamatini.

Letter, after letter, "I adore you" ,"Please never leave me", "I'm madly in love with you", "You take my breath away", "If I had not done what I did, you could have loved me." That last one caught my attention. I looked at that sentence over and over again. A sensation of something more lying within the text and I was unable to shake it from me. To be honest I was skimming most of the graphics of the letters because I didn't want to read all the ways people wanted my brother, but this one stood out to me. I read the letter thoroughly.

From: Your Secret Admirer

To: My Love Sebastien

I see you day in and day out. I wish I could be as close to you at night as the covers on your bed, and pillow to your head. The thought of you torments me every second from dusk to dawn. Every day I see you lost in thought in the garden writing in your journal. Am I in there somewhere? Am I so foolish to think I would ever have a place in your thoughts as you do in mine. Sometimes I wonder if what I am doing is even worth it. If I had not done what I did, you could have loved me.

Sincerely,, YOur Secret Admirer 

"Who could this be? They clearly did something they weren't supposed to." I said showing mom who was sitting at a table in Ms. Alma's class. It seems we've been finding ourselves in this room often, lately.

Looking at the letter, "Every day I see you lost in thought in the garden writing in your journal."

Continuing to read aloud, "If I had not done what I did, you could have loved me."

I looked at her wondering if she had any hunches about the letter.
"So, what do you think?" still looking at her.

"It does sound odd. But we could be trying to read into it because we're hoping to find a clue." She said returning the letter.

"I don't know, I feel like this one is a bit suspicious. " I responded and took back the letter.

Mom may not have had her hunches on this letter, but I felt strongly about it. I decided to keep the letter to look into it more in depth. Putting the letter in my pocket, "Mom, can't you just have one of your visions and find out where Liriden is? That would make this go so much faster...." Apparently I had spoken too soon. When I looked back at mom from putting the letter in my pocket, she seemed to be in a trance. It looked similar to that day at the house when she made everything go crazy. But this time it felt different, her hair wasn't floating. She was sitting up straight. Her eyes with that pale ghostly look to them.

"Mom? Hey mom? Are you having a vision?" I asked.
She didn't respond. She just looked straight out in the distance. I noticed at the corner of her eyes, neon white little veins were appearing. I didn't like how this was looking, especially since she wasn't responding. Reaching out and touching her shoulder to snap her out of it, "Mom! Snap out of it! Hey mom!" I said getting a bit concerned.

All of a sudden she blinked. But when I looked into her eyes , they weren't her eyes I was looking at. It was someone else's. Mom with dark green eyes, she smiled at me, "You poor thing. You're looking in the wrong place, Little Princess." She spoke to me, in another voice. The voice of an old woman.

Quickly realizing the person now speaking to me was not my mother, I jolted my hand back to myself, "Who are you?" , I asked.

Getting up to look around, now with a hunch in her back and a limp in her step, she began to look at the papers that were still laid out on the table. I wasn't sure if she had heard me, so I repeated myself. "Who are you?" I said with a more stearness in my voice.

Whipping her look towards me and slowly smiling, " Do not worry child, I do not plan to stay long. You are just like your mother, you know. Witty and quick to solve puzzles,"she said, looking for something amongst the paper.

"Ah-ha! Here it is." She gave me one of the papers that mom had in an old book.
"One thing about your mother that never changes, she always has the answer right in front of her,"she said, giving me the paper.

I cautiously and suspiciously took the paper from her. It was a very old paper. It had a cloth-like texture that didn't have any writing on it. Feeling confused, I looked at the women that clearly possessed my mother at the moment.

"I don't understand. This is an empty piece of paper. How is this an answer? And how do you know my mother?" I asked a bit anxiously.

"Oh Little Princess, If we had all the answers at hand, life would be so boring. Don't you think?.......But I will say this, look deep into who you are and you'll find the way. When you're trying to be someone you are not, you get blinded by what isn't, instead of focusing on what is," she ended.

"I feel like you just threw a lot of riddles at me, instead of just telling me straight forward what to do with this," I responded unamused.

She chuckled, " Little Princess, this paper is not empty. Look at it and tell me what you see?"

"Little Princess, I've heard that before from one person only. My great great grandmother used to call me that." I thought aloud.

Looking at her, I realized it was her, at least her spirit. But why did she choose to appear now? And why possess my mom's body? These were all questions I would have loved to get the answer to but it seemed I was running out of time with the line connection.

Trying to refocus on the task at hand, I stared at the paper and attempted to concentrate. "What.....the ......Fu.." I couldn't even finish my last word. As I stared at the paper, words began to appear. I couldn't make a clear picture of what it was saying because all of the words were out of order.

“It seems like there's words revealing themselves to me, “ I said, looking at the page and then looking at her.

She smiled and then sat back down, took a deep breath, blinked once, twice and her green eyes turned to those soft coffee brown eyes. Those eyes belonged to mom.

“Uhhhhh.....mom?” I asked curiously and reassured myself it was in fact mom who I was now speaking to.

“Yes?” She responded.

“I found a potential answer to our problems, well current problem.” I said as I showed her the paper.

“Uhm, Reina, Sweety, there’s nothing on here.” She responded by returning the paper.

“Yes, there is! Look harder.” I gave her the paper again to look at.

Taking the paper back, she stared intensely at the paper. Within a few seconds her eyes began to widen, but then a wrinkled glabella appeared between her eyebrows.

"What's wrong?" I asked.
"It 's all out of order." She said, still staring at the paper.
" Well that's something we need to figure out together." I took the paper back and began to examine the sheet and the location of the words. I noticed that some words were written in a different penmanship and some letters were larger than the others.

"Look, these words are bigger than the rest. And these are written differently. As if there was more than one person who wrote on this paper." I pointed at the words and letters while showing mom." *This writing seems almost familiar, I thought to myself.*

"Hmmmm.... it's a code." My mom said as she quickly pulled out a notebook that was sitting on the mess that was on the table.

"T...h...e...y...r...e...c...o....m...i...n...g...f...o ...r... y..o..u", She wrote on the paper.

"They're coming for you?" I read aloud. "Well that's fucking creepy." I continued, "Who is?" I looked at mom to ask, maybe she might have an answer. And as usual she did, but it wasn't the one I was expecting.

"Well I don't know but, there's more here." She said, and continued to write.

"L....0....C...K ..3...R...6...4" Mom put her pen down to pick up the sheet. "Locker 64?" She asked as she looked up at me.

"Maybe we have to go to locker 64?" I said, trying to solve the puzzle.

"But this school no longer uses the lockers. They are all on the 4th floor. Which is commonly used as a storage floor. Mom was easily able to get the keys to the 4th floor from Mr. Loyd. She had told him it was important that she get on the 4th floor, it was in one of her visions. This was a white lie, but anyways we proceeded on the search.

It wasn't but ten minutes later we made our way to the lockers on the 4th floor. It was like a maze of tall lockers up there. It took us a while to find Locker 64, but we finally found it. The blue color that it was painted seemed to have faded away. It was rusted and made a squeaky noise when we tried to open it.

“The door is jammed.” I said as I struggled to open it.
“Let me see.” Mom gave it a tug and a yank.

KA-CLANK

Mom managed to unjam the locker. As it slowly opened we found nothing but cobwebs and dirt marks on the bottom.

“This can’t be it.” Mom said.

“Let me see the paper.” I said, reaching for the notebook paper mom had ripped from the notebook she wrote on earlier.

“L0CK3R64”, I thought about how she wrote it all.
“I think there’s a code, within a code. Look, the way you wrote Locker. You used two numbers in the word. Maybe it’s not locker 64….but locker 0364.” I said looking at her.

"That's not a locker on this floor. That's a locker in the basement." Mom said slowly, taking the paper back in thought.

As we made our way down to the basement we came across what felt like twins since the third had been apart from Lyla and Lumiere for what felt like so long. I informed them on the potential lead to finding their third half. When we finally got to the basement, the hall doors to the space were unlocked. Between the four of us, we were able to find this locker a lot faster than the one that we had searched for on the 4th floor.

"Here it is!" Lyla shouted with excitement.

We all approached the locker. Mom, eager to open it, gave it a shove and a yank. And nothing, she wasn't able to open this locker the same way she did earlier. Lumiere thought that he would be able to open it and gave it a try and still no success.

"Let me try." Lyla said.

And with no avail, the locker stood shut. I decided to give it a shot. Putting all my strength and energy into opening this locker, I yanked, bang and shoved like a maniac, and nothing. It stood shut. And then I thought, let me try with my Teolt, I have been practicing and have been getting better at controlling it.

“Okay, I am going to try to open it with my Teolt.” I stated.
“Oh lord, take cover. The whole place may crumble on us.” Lumiere teased.
“Lumiere, don’t make fun of your sister. At least she’s trying to help.” Mom said as she pushed the two of them back.

“Seriously mom.” I said, noticing they were slowly taking cover.
“Hey it can’t hurt us to want to be safe.” She said as she pointed with her lips towards the locker, notioning me to open it.

“Alright! Here goes nothing.” I said as I concentrated on the locker door.
Feeling the door and the material it was made of, along with everything else around me, I could hear the screws and metal begin to crunch into itself and begin to vibrate. It was as if it was resisting in a way, but it wasn’t able to hold on to the body of the locker anymore. And with that the door went flying straight between the twins and my mom, grazing Lumiere on the shoulder.

“Ouch!” he shouted.
“Oh my goodness! Are you ok?” I asked, concerned that I had severely hurt him. When I looked closer, the graze was not bigger than a papercut.
“Bruh.” I said, looking at him like, are you serious.

Pouting at me while holding his arm, “I’m fine I guess.” Lumiere said as he looked at the doorless locker. “What is that?” he asked, still holding his arm.

All of us looked at each other and then approached the locker where an old book was lying at the bottom with a note attached to it.

I'm Sorry

Lyla read out loud as she picked up the book.
A

Taking the book from her, mom said we needed to continue this in Ms.Alma’s Classroom. So we made our way up and all sat down at another table next to the one that had a mess on it. All of us were nervous to find what lied in this old book, and curious to why there was a note that said I’m Sorry.

Mom cracked open the book, and began to read it aloud to us. This story was written in a way that seemed like a journal but told a tale at the same time. The story line seemed odd,as if it was eternal, or went on a never ending loop. The entries began in the 1400's. The first five journal entries told a tale of a King and a Queen, and their baby boy that they loved very much. They had encountered an oracle that had told them their son would be a great, strong and powerful leader one day and that he would go through trials and tribulations that only he can pass on his own. The parents weren't too concerned since the oracle had said he would be strong and powerful. That he would be gifted with the power of the Gods. And so it came to be that their son was exactly as the oracle said at the age of 12.

The following year from the son's 12th birthday they had another child, a baby girl. And so they summoned the oracle again. The oracle was older now and not as strong, but he obliged the King and Queen.

" This child will be a great leader. She will be beautiful and kind." The oracle told the King and Queen.

"But the gift! What of the gift?" The king and queen were eager to know. What great strengths will they have in addition to their kingdom.

A bit disappointed by the thirst for power the oracle told them that she would have the gift of a Goddess and that they will find out as soon as she reaches mature age.

Not but a few years later, they had their third child, another boy. And again they summoned the oracle.

The oracle was much older. Now with long gray hair, and a tired wrinkled face.

The King and Queen asked, "what of this child? What great power will they possess?"

The oracle told them that he would lead soldiers into battle and come out triumphant, "he would have a great heart even through the sights he will see within the battlefield. This may or may not be his downfall."

The king was disappointed and asked about the gift, "what will he have?"

The oracle looked at the king and queen and said "What better gift than to have a great heart?"

The king was not pleased with this and told the oracle he demanded to know. He claimed the oracle to be holding back the truth and locked him up until he gave him the truth he seeked. The oracle died after a few years in the dungeon with all types of bruises and marks, from the king ordering his men to force out the answer.

The king went on a rampage in search of more oracles. And each told him the same thing until one day, he came across an old woman oracle. She told him the same thing but with a twist at the end.

"....Yes, a great heart. But a gift from the gods? No, I don't think so. Just a nice lad, with a great heart. He will concur..." And before she could finish the king stabbed her through the stomach leaving her in shock. She said he was a fool, cursing him to live all of his lives in an endless loop and never getting to know...." Mom ended and looked at us.

"Know what?" Lyla and Lumiere synchronically said.

"That's where it ends." Mom responded and gently closed the old book. She carried this intense look in her face.

"What's wrong? Why do you have that face?" I asked as I began to get up from my seat.

"Something just doesn't seem right." She responded.
"What's right about any of this?" I sassed.

Mom looked at me unamused. She got up from her seat and walked to the table where the mess of papers and documents still lay.

She leaned over reaching for a sheet that was hidden under the mess of paper. Slowly pulling it out of underneath, she turned towards us.

"This sheet of paper was not here earlier." Mom said as she looked at the paper and then at us.

Walking towards her to take the paper. And again, that penmanship, I have seen it before,I just couldn't put my finger on where. I can feel frustration coming over me because we continue to go at such a slow pace.

"Agh! We're never going to find him Mom!" I yelled.

"Don't say that. We just need to focus a little more." Mom responded.

All of a sudden Lumiere and Lyla's stomach began to rumble loudly.

“Have you guys not eaten or something, because that was abnormally loud.” I looked at the two.

“I don’t think it’s our hunger.”Lyla said, looking at everyone with a dismal look.
“I think they are starving him.” Lumiere said as he matched Lyla’s dismal expression.

“Okay, Okay, you guys go eat. Eat for three people. Apparently this is a pain you guys share. It probably won't feed him but the energy and nutrients will be shared. And Reina, I’m pretty sure you have a class that will be starting soon. Go to class. We need to come back with fresh eyes and energy.” Mom said as she scrambled to think of different plans and ideas to save her triplets and not lose her head doing so.

Lyla and Lumiere did as they were told. I went to my third class. This class was my 3rd class and I have been dodging it for a while. Especially since Adonis is in that class, he really makes me feel uneasy for some reason. The first time I went into the class and saw him, he gave me a mischievous smile on his face as if he knew he created discomfort for me. But I couldn’t keep missing this class. I feel like I’d only be taking away from my own education. Even if it is a gym class. Still having the triplets in the back of my head and everything that happened earlier, I couldn't seem to focus.

Finally, walking into what seemed like the biggest gym I have ever seen, I saw a crowd of students in gym clothing. This has to be the easiest class, I thought to myself. And just as quickly as I thought it, my opinion changed when I saw someone flung across the room by a big ass plant. Drawing my attention to where the flung body came from I saw a 5ft lady laughing with a sense of success. Looking back at the flung body, now getting up from the giant gymnastic beds.

"Leif?" I said as I walked towards him.

"Reina! Hey!" He said with excitement in his voice.

"Heyyy, what are you doing flying across the room? Last I remember, that wasn't exactly your gift." I joked.

"Ah, yeah I was placed in this class to help me practice and "exercise" my gift." He said as he rubbed his back that seemed to be in pain.

"DelaRosa! You are up!" A voice shouted out from the crowd of students.
Looking at the group, and feeling confused as to who called out my name. In the middle stood a voluptuous woman in a tracksuit.

"Doukas! She shouted again, "You're up with DelaRosa!"

I looked at Leif confused. "What is she talking about?" I asked.
"This is a class to exercise your gift. Seems like you have .... Doukas." He pointed to a familiar looking guy,Adonis, in the middle of the gym that seemed to be waiting for me. Still confused on how this game goes I walked up to the space that was provided to me, leaving me now standing ten feet away from him.

"Dookie, huh?" I said making fun of Adonis's last name.
He smiled with that mischievous smile again, as if he had his prey where he wanted it. He began to rub his middle and index finger with his thumb.

All of a sudden, he began to charge at me so quickly, I didn't realize how fast he caught up to me. With the same hand he was rubbing his fingers he touched me slightly on my shoulder, sending me into one of his lustful trances, allowing me to see him holding and gently kissing the top of my hand while dragging his lower lip up to my wrist. I could hear his voice in a whisper saying, "Doukas....Adonis Doukas...".

Being able to snap out of his trance, I found myself now laying flat on my back.

When did I fall back?I thought to myself. Sitting up brushing myself off, I looked at him. He now stood 5 ft away. As he looked down at me, he had a sense of being surprised again.

"That was not supposed to happen. It was supposed to last longer." He said looking around as if he was searching for someone to acknowledge the fact that the trance was supposed to last longer.

I, still sitting on the floor, raised my right arm and made a gun shape with my fingers, aimed it at him and began to feel everything around me again. Everything began to tremble.

"Don't kill him Reina." Suddenly Gio's Voice appeared.

"Gio? Are you in this class, I didn't see you?" I responded telepathically while looking

around to search for my brother, but still focused on Adonis.

"*No, but your thoughts are so loud I can hear them three classrooms away.*" Gio said.

"*So you want me to let him just do what he wants and not fight back?*" I asked a bit in disbelief.

"*I didn't say that, I said don't kill him. Knock that guy on his ass.*" Gio ended.

Still with my gun hand pointing at Adonis and a smile slowly curling on my face, I breathed in and I breathed out. The tremors were still going but slightly easing due to my breathing pace. Just when I was calm enough not to kill someone, I shot a blast at Adonis.

BOOM! A sound wave appeared from the force.

He jolted back to one of the giant gym beds.

And he didn't get up.

Chapter Nine

"Diving in Deep"

Well, Adonis didn't die that day. But he definitely was sent to the emergency room on campus for a week. I wonder if the blow was enough for him to learn to stop toying with me and leave me alone.

It's been another week that we haven't found Liriden, and it's becoming harder on Lyla and Lumiere to exist in general. They look as if a piece of their soul has parted from them. Their lips are commonly a more purple tone, skin has become more pale and they constantly have the shivers. But they always have the same sense of humor.

The clocks anywhere I went seemed to sound loud to me, as if the clock was letting me know with every strike we were running out of time.

With the time that had passed. Leif and I have become closer with each other. So much so, I eventually felt comfortable enough to share with him what has been on my mind and going on with the family.

We were in a study room in the campus library, when I had told him, working on an assignment that Mr. Gregor gave us about "Diving in Deep" into our emotions and triggers. We're supposed to do some research on possibilities and write a two page paper on it. Which I thought was a piece of cake till I remembered those who have two ethnicities have to look in two different directions. I had to look in several varieties of text books to read more on both of my ethnic and cultural background. It was all very fascinating so I wasn't too bothered by it.

As I was working in the study room with Leif, I had moments where I couldn't focus. It was because I had been thinking about our missing member of the family.

"Hey.....everything ok?" Leif asked as he highlighted a part of a paragraph in a text book.

"Um, aren't you supposed to return that? And I'm fine." I said, spinning my pen back and forth in the air with my right hand.

"Are you sure?" He pushed for a better answer.

"Mhmm," I said, nodding my head once.

He looked at me in silence for a second,"....You've been distracted a lot lately Reina....don't think I have not noticed... I think we've hung out together long enough for me to see you're clearly in and out of this space mentally."

I took a deep breath, and looked at him. I can feel myself letting my worry come to surface.
"I....I've been going through some things lately...."I began to tell him.

"What do you mean?" He asked as he closed his highlighter.

"A lot of things, actually." I continued.

Part of me wanted to just bluntly tell him , but for some reason I couldn't help but want to hold back. Was this fear? Am I feeling scared?A moment passed before I could continue. Then I realized it was a type of fear. It was a fear of opening up and letting someone else in,again.

He put his highlighter down, and clasp his hands together letting me know he is fully listening. I took another deep breath, and let go in hope that this one will stay. I began with how I really came to be at the Campus. How I had accidentally unleashed a wave of my power on Tim,and then gradually led up to the present day events.

" And....you know how you've met my siblings?...." I asked.

"Yes?" Leif said questionably as he leaned forward.

"And the Triplets?" I continued.

He chuckled, "You mean twins." Leif said with a smile.

I looked at him, feeling the sadness coming over me. Lost in thought on the fact that I might go home and see Lyla and Lumiere lifeless.

"No.......Triplets", I said again.

He tilted his head confused.

“I have Triplet siblings, they’re kind of a package deal. All or nothing.” I smile recalling silly memories of them.

“So…who is the third one?...Don’t tell me Sebastien.” He joked.
“The third one…his name is Liriden, is really sweet and mostly quiet…..but he can get sassy sometimes and show it on his face.” I said as I began to smile.

“Seems like you love your siblings a lot.” He said as he began to look at me and then back to his paper. “So where is he?” He asked as he picked up his highlighter again.

“Missing.” I said. “He’s missing, and has been since about the time I arrived here.” I said slowly putting my pen down from fidgeting with it.

“What?? That’s a long time to be missing, did you file a police report?”Leif asked.
“And tell them something supernatural took my brother and is torturing him?” I said sarcastically.
Leif sat back in what looked like shock.
“How do you know it’s supernatural and that they are torturing him?” He asked.

"Because he's linked to Lyla and Lumiere." I responded.

Leif stood quiet for a moment, as if he was now lost in thought. His face got very serious and with a somewhat bothersome facial expression. He leaned forward again.

"I'll help you find him. Liriden , was his name right?" He asked.

"Yes." I said, feeling a bit of hope that another person on the search for Liriden will speed up the timeline.

After our conversation Leif offered to take me home since it was Friday, I didn't really need to stay over on Campus. I agreed to it, since everyone else was busy and I didn't want to do that journey home alone.

"Is it ok, if we take the fast route?" Leif asked.

"What do you mean, 'Fast Route'?" I asked, confused.

He began to get close to me with a soft smile, and gently put his arm around me.

"Hey man, if you're going to take me the *'Fast Route'*, at least take me on a date first." I said taking a step away from him.

He chuckled, "Relax, the 'Fast Route' is me traveling with my power. It gets me places faster." Leif said, showing me his palms, so as to not give me the wrong idea.

"Have you done this before?" I asked as I walked towards him in a slight agreement.

"Absolutely!" He said holding me close with his arms wrapped around my waist.

"Your arms are a bit low." I told him as I lifted one of my eyebrows.

He began to slowly raise them.

"So, who have you done this before with?" I asked, still a bit unsure of what we're going to do.

"A teddy bear." He said smiling.

"A TEDDY BEA!..." And before I could even finish we poofed into thin air and were now at the parking lot by the forest preserve before all the walking to get to the gate.

I Gasped aggressively, taking a few steps away from him. I felt as if I was under water and couldn't breathe during the teleportation, and when we appeared, so did the oxygen.

"What the fuck was that!" I attempted to yell, still trying to catch my breath.

"Oh , yeah, I forgot to mention to hold your breath. When we 'disappear' we are technically and literally turning into thin air, so the matter and particles all around us goes in and out of us, unless you hold your breath. I don't know why, it's just something that seems to work.....at least for me." He said casually.

Upset that he just threw me in a whirl wind and didn't think to inform me on these important details, I walked up to him and punched him on his chest.

"Owww! What was that for?" Leif asked, rubbing the spot where I had just hit him.

I looked at him a bit bothered for the lack of common sense he clearly seems to have at this very moment.

"Sooooooooo, do you want to teleport to your house?" He asked,a bit frightened at what my response might be.

"I think I had enough teleportation for today, thank goodness our car is right here and I was smart enough to bring the keys." I said as I walked up to the car to open it.

"Do you still want me to go with you...?" He asked.

"If you go with me, how will you get back?" I asked.

He chuckled and then teleported into the passenger seat. Then, I understood that he was perfectly capable of finding his way back to campus, or wherever he needed to go. I inhaled and exhaled; walking around the car and got in the driver's seat. I reversed and began to go on my way home.

Once I arrived, I decided to invite him into my house. As I walked in I saw Lumiere on the couch playing a game on his phone.

"Hey, Lumi!" I said, as I closed the door behind Leif and I.But I didn't get a response.

"Lumi! Hello?!" I greeted him again, walking towards him.

"Ahh!" Lumi shouted, startled by my presence. "How long have you been here??" He asked.

"Bro....seriously?" I reached to grab his left hearing aid from his ear . "Have you charged these?" I asked, noticing he was staring at my lips movement.

"Oh, yeah I forgot to charge it." He said as he took the hearing aid back.

Shaking my head, I went to a drawer by the Living room computer desk and pulled out a set of hearing aids that mom had put to charge. She had specifically told me to remember their location. I guess she saw this coming.

Handing them to him and taking the other ones to charge it, I couldn't help notice the silence in the house.

"Are you the only one here?" I asked as I looked around and towards the staircase.

"Well, mom is upstairs trying to see information that she demands through her visions, but we all know that's not how that works. And.... Sebastien went on one of his journeys with AzaRayah. She told him it would be better if we split up and supposedly *cover more grounds* to find some more answers on the old book we had found in the locker. She said that she knows someone that could help in Italy."

"Ita...Why Italy!? And she couldn't call them!?" I felt off about what Lumiere just told me, but maybe it's just me, still suspicious about anyone who gets close to my family. But in Italy, that means he had to take a plane to get there. So he is wasting time not looking for Liriden.

"Okay.........and how about everyone else?" I asked, trying not to react too much to the fact that Sebastien allowed himself to think traveling to Italy in a time like this was a good idea.

" Gio has been with his Girlfriend the majority of today and most days this past week. So he might be with her." He said as he began to get up from the couch.

"And Evan, well she's been keeping to herself lately. She said she was going to campus to do some *Light Reading*. I told her 'yeah fucking right, Light Reading my Ass. You go through ten chapter books in fifteen minutes and call it *Light Reading*.' But whatever, Oh hey Leif! I didn't notice you standing there." He ended, looking at Leif who was looking around where he stood.

Refocusing his gaze on Lumiere, Leif responded, "Dude...you're deaf, not blind." .

Lumiere smiled mischievously, " I guess you are right, I just thought I'd acknowledge you." Lumiere laughed.

All of a sudden the house began to tremble. Lumiere and I looked at each other a bit concerned and we quickly hurried up the stairs to mom's room. Somehow we had a feeling this had something to do with her. Leif followed us up the stairs. She was sitting on her bed staring into the abyss,like she does when she's in one of her trances.

""Ocama...... Boya.....Guerico......Bara Bajacu. " Mom began to mutter. "Ocama.....Boya Guerico......Bara.....Bajacu...."She continued.

"Mom, what are you saying?" I asked, in hope she could still hear me in her trance.

"Maybe she wants to go to Bora Bora?" Lumiere said.

Unamused, I looked at him, " I don't think that's what she wants, Lumiere." I responded.

"Well it's worth a try." He replied.

"I've heard her say these words before. It was one of the first few days when I first arrived back home." I told Leif and Lumiere.

"Mom, tell me what you're trying to say." I said as I touched her shoulder.

Moving her gaze from the abyss to me, she stopped talking for a brief moment. I was feeling a bit unsettled, not really sure what to expect. Out of nowhere, she began to scream and yell while continuing to look me in the eyes. Her eyes looked familiar but they weren't her eyes. The screams and yelling was so frightening, that I and Lumiere jumped back, and Leif poofed into the hallway.

"Why is she screaming?!" Lumiere shouted.

"I don't know!" I shouted back.

The house was still trembling but not as aggressively like the day she received the stone from Sebastien.

Leif walked back into the room and looked at us, still frightened.

"Can you stop her from yelling!? People are going to think we're murdering her!" Leif shouted.

"AHHHHHHH," Mom continued to scream. She began to do what looked like sign language. "What's she doing?" Leif asked.

"Please, don't do this, Please don't hurt me. Why are you doing this to me?What did I do? What did I do to you? Whatever it is.....I'm sorry...." I read what she was signing out loud. And then it clicked, maybe she wasn't signing. Maybe she was channeling,and the person she was channeling was Liriden.

Mom's eyes began to water as she returned to herself. She began to cry, feeling helpless. I rubbed her shoulder, trying to comfort her.

“What happened? You were saying those words again and then you started screaming.” I asked her.

“After truly listening ....I think I know what it is.....that our ancestors have been trying to tell me.....they said to “Listen...that an Evil Spirit will come ... .and that there will be death ... .by morning light in the native language of the Taino's.” she said as she began to wipe her teary eyes away.

“As for everything else ....I was trying to see where Liriden was but I think I was placed in his body for what felt like a split second. He was in, what looked like a giant fish tank, in this really big room. And there was someone coming....it's essence was dark and evil.” She said as she began to cry again.

“Don't worry mom, we will find him.” I said, trying to reassure her, as I looked back at Leif and Lumiere.

“Why don't you rest for a bit, it seems like that really pulled a lot of energy from you.” I continued to say as I laid her down and covered her.

I turned to Lief and Lumiere, “We need to figure something out and fast. We need to find Liriden. “ I said as I guided everyone out the room.

“Well we can go back to campus and see what we can find.” Lief suggested.

“I’ll stay here with mom to make sure she’s ok.” Lumiere said.

“Alright then , we’ll be back Lumi.” I said to Lumiere, “and keep those aids charged.” I added as I descended the staircase to head out the door with Leif.

Back on campus, Leif and I were messing around with the book and found a hidden compartment in the spine. I was standing by the table and he was sitting adjacent to me. After shaking the book gently a bit, with the opening facing down to the table, a small note came out.

“Man these people used to looooove notes, huh.” I said, grabbing the note as I looked at Leif.

"They sure did……what does it say?” he responded with a head nod upwards notioning me to read it.

"I love you! And I love him. Why can't you just accept that the child is mine!" - Your Lover

Realizing and putting the pieces together we looked at each other shocked. With just one note, I looked at Leif, "it wasn't the king's child? ....Then who was it?"

"I don't know", he responded.

"I feel that this just made me get more questions. One thing for sure though, it's more safe than not to say that the reason the child didn't have a gift was because he was from a different father. "

"But that doesn't make sense, because there are some families and people in general that don't get their abilities. Well at least in this day and age." Leif said, taking the note from me.

"Well according to Ms.Cuapa, some generations get skipped by the millenia." I responded as I sat next to him.

He put the note down on the table and looked at me, "Hey, let's take a break from this. You look like you need a break, have you eaten?"

I let out a big exhale "They are going to kill him, Leif. And the others of the triplets are going to feel as if it was their own death.....They won't ever be the same again. We are all for the most part trying our best to find him." I said as I rested my head into both my palms.

I felt his hand gently placed on my back, "we're going to find him." Leif looked at me with the most sincere face and determination.

Leif and I eventually wrapped things up that day and I went home. When I arrived home Evan was sitting on one of the couches in the living room with her legs up on the couch. She was doing something on her phone. I didn't even bother to talk to her, she would only get on my nerves. I made my way past the living room and began to head up the stairs, just to feel a sudden breeze of air and abruptly stopped by her at the top of the stairs.

Looking at me with an intense squint in silence, she took a deep breath and stepped aside. Confused, I looked at her and continued up, taking a quick glance at her once more before walking into my room.

I wonder what that was about, I thought to myself. I sat on my bed to take a moment and just breathe. Things are getting crazy around here and on campus. I honestly feel like shit's not going to get better here on out, thinking to myself, I threw myself to lay back on my bed.

"TING"

My phone went off. I wasn't going to answer it, but ...

"TING"

Again, it went off, letting me know I had another notification.

"Ahhhhhh, okay... okay, let me see what's going on."

I gasped! It was Liriden! Confused but glad to hear from him I responded rapidly.

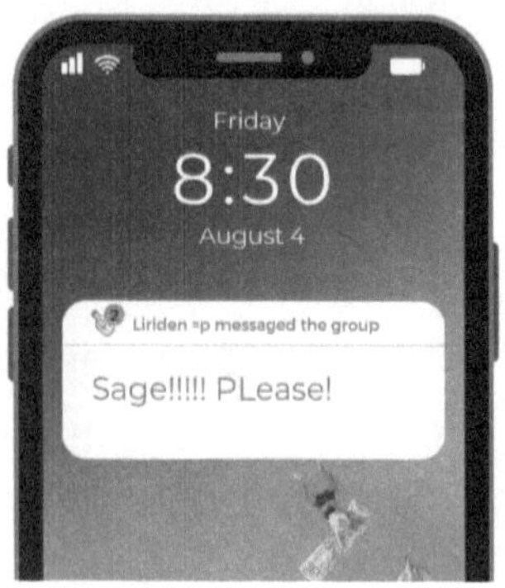

Reina
Where are you?

Lyla
Liriden! Where r you?

Lumi
Tell us where you are!

Gio
Guys, let him talk.

Apparently, I wasn’t the only one.

We all met in the living room that evening in hope to hear back from Liriden, even Evan was there. It’s been half an hour since we’ve heard anything. We began to grow impatient and anxious.

“Why hasn’t he responded yet?” Lyla asked.
“Maybe he can’t?” Evan said.

“Wait a minute…”, Lumiere’s face lit up so bright, you would think his head was going to pop off. “What?” Gio asked.

“He has his phone…has anyone tried tracking his phone?” Lumiere got up and walked over to the family computer that sat on a fairly old desktop in the corner of the living room.

“Well I did, but it only gave me the last location he was when he last messaged the group.” Lyla said as she followed Lumiere towards the computer.

“Well he messaged recently so his location should be updated.” Lumiere said as he began to track Liridens phone.

The curiosity and eagerness to find our brother pulled all of us towards the computer as well. We waited impatiently for a result. And in just a few seconds, we had his location.

Chapter Ten

"A night to Remember"

We found that his phone was traced to an address about an hour away. After looking up the address, we were determined to see and know where and what this house looked like. Seeing that it was an old manor but an hour away, we quickly rushed to go out the door. Just before reaching for the door knob, Evan zoomed in front of us to stop us.

"What are you doing?! Let us through!" Lumiere and Lyla shouted at her.
"Have any of you *Dipwods* ever stopped to think this might be a trap?" She asked.
"Even if it was, we probably can take whoever it is on and still save Liriden." Lumiere said.

Shaking her head she responded, " You guys need to think more strategically and not just jump into a wolf's den." She stepped aside.

Taking into consideration what she said they looked at her and at one another then back at Gio and I.

"Well we can go drive by it and see what we are working with?" Gio said.
This brightened Lyla and Lumiere's face.

So we did just as Gio suggested. We drove the hour to this manor during the evening. We had thought it would be a better time of day since the sun would be setting and we could blend in a little better. When we arrived we could see the finely trimmed bushes and a tall fence that required a code to access the inside grounds of the manor. Lumiere and Lyla were using binoculars to see better.

"What....where did you guys get those?" I asked, surprised by the binoculars' random appearance.
"What? You don't carry a set of binoculars with you at all times?" Lumiere responded.

“Yeah Reina, how come you don’t carry a set of binoculars with you at all times?” Gio joked.

I looked at him unamused, “No Gio, do you ?” I sassed back.

“Shhhhhhhhhh, someone is coming!” Lyla shouted.
“Why are you yelling, when you are telling us to shush!” Evan snapped.
Lyla smiled nervously, “oh yeah, I got excited. But , look.” Lyla pointed to the fence entrance.

It was ...Dina. She was parting from the entrance and saying her farewells to an older man that looked like he was in his mid to late 50’s.

“Look! There’s someone else walking to the gate.” Gio said.
“Wait ....isn’t that your professor,Reina? Professor Gregor was it?” Gio continued.

“That is him, but what is he doing here?” I asked aloud.
“Alright guys, I think we’ve seen enough to plan. We’ll come back once we are prepared.” Evan said as she started the car and headed home.

We planned multiple plans that night and the following day, just so we aren't unprepared. It was Monday when we had finalized the official plan. Sebastien was still on his way back from Italy, he had said the person AzaRayah had suggested no longer lived there.

I was lost in thought as I sat at the table that I shared with Leif in Professor Gregors class. I couldn't help but stare at him and wonder what he was doing at that manor. The Manor that my brother was being tortured at. And why was Dina there?

"Hey, you good?" Leif asked.

"Huh? Um…Yeah. All good." I said as I detached my glare from the professor to set it onto Leif. "Okay, well I know this isn't the best time but ….I was invited to something and I'm able to bring a plus one. And…I was wondering if you'd like to go with me? I know it's a bit short notice." He smiled.

"I don't know Leif, this isn't…." Before I finished he showed me the invitation.

“Look! It’s tomorrow at 8pm, it’s only about 2 hours. It’s a Gala.” He said with hope in his voice.

I took the invitation to look at it. My heart dropped when I saw the address. It was the address of the manor we’ve been planning to break into, to save Liriden.

“You don’t have to go if you really don’t want to?” Leif said as he took the invitation back.

After a brief moment to think and a second to come up with an idea, I quickly responded, “You know what.... I think I’d like to go.” I said with a slight smile. I thought about the fact that Leif didn’t know about the address ,yet. But most of all why was he invited to this Manor?

“Really!” Leif shouted in high pitch with excitement. After realizing his high pitch he regulated his voice and continued to say, “,....Awesome, That’s cool. I’ll pick you up at 7pm, if that’s ok?”

“Alright,I’ll see you then.” I attempted to say with happy excitement.

“ All right everyone, unfortunately class is going to be shortened today. I have an important meeting to attend. But before I do that .....Reina, please stay after class for a moment. Everyone else is dismissed.”

Leif and I looked at each other a little confused. Everyone cleared out of the classroom, but Leif didn’t leave this time, he decided to stay. Mr.Gregor looked at him, “Don’t you have somewhere to be Leif”.

“Yeah, I am just waiting for Reina.” Leif responded as he smiled at Professor Gregor.

“Well this matter doesn’t concern you, so can you please wait outside” Professor Gregor said in a stern voice.

They both stared intensely at each other for what felt like forever. Glaring at Professor Gregor, Leif touched my shoulder before leaving the classroom and said, “I’ll wait for you in the hall”

After Professor Gregor basically walked Leif out the class, he closed the door behind Leif. Leaving it to be just him and I in the classroom.

"So you wanted to talk to me?" I asked as I fidgeted with the spine of a notebook I had in front of me on the table.

"Yes, I couldn't help but notice your burning glare on me in the time we were in class. Is there something wrong?" He said as he leaned back on another table facing me with his arms crossed.

"No, nothing's wrong, perfectly fine." I said as I got up and gathered my things.

I can feel him now staring at me, "You know it's rude to not look someone in the eye when they're talking to you?" He said.

Tearing my eyes from my things I looked at him in his intense blue eyes, and I could feel my jaw clench.

"Professor Gregor, I just had something on my mind. It was something that had happened in another class, I guess I zoned out on you and that's what you were feeling." I said as I tried to believe my own white lie for this second.

"Alright then, if that's all it was, you are free to go. I apologize for delaying your schedule." He got up from the table he was leaning on and walked over to his desk .

Relief that he swallowed my white lie ,I tried to calmly leave the class but according to Leif it was more as if I scurried out the door.

“So what was that all about?” Leif asked.

“Nothing major, the real question here is what the fuck is up with you and Mr. Gregor?Why is there always some type of tension between you two?” I asked Leif.

He stood quiet for a moment, “ I don’t know, it’s been a thing since I met him. He undermines me a lot and he thinks he’s better than everyone and the Man doesn’t even have powers. You know he’s only like 4 or 5 years older than us right? “ Leif said as he shook his head in disapproval.

“He’s What!!?” I shouted in shock, “Well I guess that explains why he looks so young and attractive. Also he’s really mature.”

“Yeah, I know. Many of the ladies in our class swoon for him, I don’t know why…the man’s not even all that.” He said as we made our way towards the entrance of the building.

"Are you jealous?" I asked.

Leif scuffed," Me? Jealous? Please Reina, don't offend me; Anyway, I have some things to do before tomorrow so I'm going to skip the rest of the classes for today. I'll see you tomorrow." He said as he parted ways with me to leave. After he left I headed to finish what was left of my schedule.

Looking at my watch I decided to think a little more about my new plan. I texted the sibling group chat to let everyone know that I will be going to the Manor as an invite to a Gala, so we had a foot in the door. Everyone agreed it was the smoothest and least criminal way to get into this Manor. Lumiere was disappointed that he wasn't going to be able to burn a hole through one of the side windows. I did tell them that I wanted them to stand by just in case the shit hits the fan.

The next day after all my classes, I went home to prepare for *Mission Liri*. I went shopping at our Local shops in town. In doing so I found myself crossing paths with Theo. I had a plan at hand so I tried to keep things brief.

“Reina! Hey! It’s been a while!” Theo shouted as he threw his arms around me.

“Theo! How’s it going!?” I asked excitedly but trying not to lose focus of the time frame we have.

“It’s been good! What are you doing here?” He said as he took a step back from me.

“I can ask the same thing haha and I am buying a dress.” I said as I showed him the cart that was filled with three dazzling Gala dresses.

“ Wow! Where are you going? “Theo asked, noticing they were in fact Gala dresses, he continued, ”And well you know my sister is having Homecoming soon, so…” He smiled.

“That’s awesome! Also, I was invited to a Gala and so I need a dress, I am actually running late so I have to let you go.” I said as I touched his arm to part ways.

“Oh okay, we should get together some time.” He said just before I turned to leave.

"Absolutely, keep in touch Theo!" I said in a rush as I went to go and check out at the cash register.

I looked at all three, there was an Ivy Green dress, a Marine Blue one and a Maroon Dress. I only had enough for one dress and a pair of heels. Ever since I started that one day a week part time job, I began to make some money. But barely, I made $65 last paycheck. I really didn't want to overwhelm myself, especially with everything that was going on. So, I decided on the Maroon dress. Mom always said that I wear the color well. I paid for my Items and went straight home.

Looking at myself now dressed up, hair done in an updo, my make up done and some borrowed dangling earrings from mom, I thought aloud, "Well this is as good as it's going to get for tonight's mission." Just as I finished saying that Evan knocked on my door.

"Well you look nice." She said as she entered.

"Is that a compliment? Am I going to die today?" I said sarcastically

.

She smiled, “Hopefully …….not…..” She looked at me with a look that I have not seen since we were kids. It was a look of hope and admiration, this lasted for a total of 2 seconds. She fixed my hair clip.

“If you need us, just let Gio know we will be but a half a mile away.” She said taking a step back to look at me better.

“I will.” As I said this I can hear Gio’s thoughts, “*He’s here*”

“Alright, the show is on.” I said as I quickly grabbed my small bag and made my way down the stairs. At the bottom of the steps was Leif In a Maroon themed suit. As I descended from the stares I couldn’t help but ask, “How did you know the color I was using?”

Leif with a look of awe and loss of words, smiled and glanced at Gio, “Mere coincidence.”

“Riiiiiiight.” I responded, “All right let's go, time is ticking.” I ended.

“Oh ….Okay” Leif said, bit taken from the sudden urge to leave.

“Sorry I have to study when I come back”,another white lie to add to the week. Why was I lying instead of telling the truth you may ask? Well, it was mainly because I couldn't help but keep thinking ……….why , why was he invited to this event and why at this Manor?

" oh, alrighty then! This way, My lady." Leif said as he opened the door for me. Making our way to the car. He then also opened the door of his car for me.

"Nice car. " I said, impressed as I entered the car.

He closed the door and poofed to the other side to the driver's door and opened it, "Thank you. I rarely use it." Leif ended as he got into the car.

"So do you know how to drive since you hardly use it?", I asked.

With the most Poker face I'd ever seen he said, " Nope!" He started the car and took off.

It wasn't till ten minutes of screaming and driving to the location that I realized he was just messing with me.

"I can't believe you did that to me." I said looking at him a little bewildered.

"Hahaha, well I don't know why you think I can't drive. But it was definitely worth watching you scream." Leif ended.

“Well that’s evil”, I said, fixing my composure.

As we went on our way we listened to music and continued casual conversations on our way to the Manor. I can see Evan’s car gradually tailing us. I felt a bit more secure knowing that they were with me.

When we finally arrived, Leif pulled up to the gate and provided the invitation to the man in what looked like a train conductor's hat. I guess the fence was opened so it was a smoother flow for the cars to enter the premises.

" Ah... welcome, Mr. Olsen and Ms. DelaRosa." The man said as he let us pass through the gate. I found myself feeling a bit anxious. The thought of getting caught in the midst of my plan was starting to creep into my subconscious. My heart is beginning to beat quickly.

And all of a sudden Gio's voice trickled into my head, "*hey relax, you're halfway there. Everything is going to be ok. Think about Liri. He needs our help.*"

I slowly regulated my breathing along with my heart rate, this allowed me to get it together. Leif reached over to hold my hand. I wonder if my anxiety was showing. I smiled to let him know I was ok. As we drove up towards the Manor there was a valet waiting to park our car.

"Mr.Olsen, Ms.DelaRosa, welcome. May I take your keys to park your vehicle?" The valet had asked Leif.

"Oh thank you." Leif said as he handed the Valet the keys.

After the entire process of getting into the building we made it to the hall that the event was being held in. On our way there, I noticed that there was a large selection of doors that were closed on both sides of the hallway but only one was slightly cracked open. Was this as Leif said, *A mere coincidence*? I wasn't certain.

We were now standing in the middle of the hall. There was lively instrumental music and hors d'oeuvres of all types. But I needed to focus, Liri is here somewhere. But where? I needed a way to escape to find him. I can always use the good old fashioned,*El baño por favor.* Will it work? Let's find out.

Before I could even try to find out whether my bathroom excuse would work, a speaker stopped the music and tapped the microphone.

Chapter Eleven

"Mirror Mirror"

Creating a small echo he began to speak,

"Hello! And Welcome to the IPWR Fundraiser! My name is Jameth McTavish, I am one of the CEO's of the IPWR corporation. Our corporation focuses on fixing the past by changing the future for the better. How do we do this exactly, you might ask? Well, let me introduce you to the founder of IPWR and he will tell you exactly what we do and are. Here is Richard Cohen!" Jameth said as he introduced Richard Cohen to the stage.

Richard Cohen, the founder of IPWR briefly explained how his company will be manufacturing machines that can predict the future. Their fundraiser will allow them to gather further materials they may need to further develop the energy machines. He vaguely explained what or how they would be powering these machines. No one seems to be too interested or concerned about it, well at least that's what it seemed like. He had said he wanted us to mainly enjoy ourselves tonight and he would be around if anyone had further questions. After his speech, the music arose again and the event was lively with conversation. I thought this would be a great time to leave. Leif had stepped away from me for a moment so I began to make my way to the *washroom*. But before I could make it to the duo doors, a familiar voice called my name.

"Ms.DelaRosa?"

As I turned to the direction of the voice I saw that 6ft tall man with black short groomed hair and intense blue eyes, in a classic royal blue paisley tuxedo. It was professor Gregor. I was surprised at how well he looked in the tux, I had to take two glances before acknowledging the fact that he called my name.

"Uh…. Ms.DelaRosa?, Professor Gregor said again.

"Ah yes, Professor Gregor, hi, how are you?" I asked, trying to take my focus from his body and outfit to his eyes.

“No different than when we last saw each other in class.” He said, flashing his charming smile at me.

“Well yeah, I suppose you’re right.” I responded.

“So, how are you here? I hope that doesn't sound wrong.” He said while reaching for a drink on a passing server who had a tray of champagne glasses.

“Well, I took this wonderful creation called a car and that is how I am here.” I said sarcastically with a slight smile.

“Ha ha, very funny, That’s not exactly what I meant but ok. I hope this isn’t too forward of me to say but, you look quite stunning in that dress tonight. Maroon really suits you. You should use it more often.” Professor Gregor said as he took a sip of his drink while he looked at me from my eyes to my toes and back. I could feel his eyes tracing my figure as he pulled his glass from his lips.

For some reason this made my cheeks begin to blush, was he flirting with me? I began to wonder. I regained my composure from the compliment that left me feeling all types of confused about him.

“No, it’s fine……..Thank you, you don’t look so bad yourself…that Navy blue becomes you. It really compliments your eyes.” I responded.

“Does it really?” He asked sarcastically, as a smile began to curl on one side of his mouth.

It was strange, at this moment I had a feeling that he was not looking at me with the same eyes of a professor, but of a man. To be honest, I couldn’t help but be drawn to the thought of it.

Catching myself, I chuckled looking down at the floor now, to then look back at him, “I’m sorry, I really need to …” before finishing my statement, Leif appeared.

“Hey, there you are!” Leif said.

As he approached me he realized who I was accompanied with and his content expression shifted to one of discontent.

“Alexander”, Leif coldly said.

"Leif", Professor Gregor reciprocated.

"Reina!" I said, trying to lighten the mood.

"I'm sorry, you will have to excuse me Reina, I have to go take care of some business. It was a pleasure seeing you here tonight, I am glad we got to socialize out of class a little." Professor Gregor bent down, took my hand and gently kissed the back of it. Lifting his head he held one last gaze into my eyes, looked at Leif and left.

Leif looked at Professor Greogor walk away, then he looked at my hand and went on to make eye contact with me.

"You should probably wash your hands, you don't know where his mouth has been," Leif said with a disgusted look.

Perfect! This is the perfect time to leave, I thought to myself. "You are absolutely right, I'll be right back." I said as I began to turn to the exit.

Finally exiting the hall, I went past the bathroom and began to snoop around into different rooms. There wasn't anyone in the hallway since they were all in the gala room. I quickly and quietly slid into a room that was dark. The only thing that lit the room was the moon light that was filtering through the window. This room looked like a library. There were a lot of books and a velvet round arm chaise by the large window.

I didn't see much here to work with so I carefully exited the room and slid into another one. I spent roughly 15 minutes doing so, until I found a room that was locked. Something felt suspicious about this, because the rest of the doors were shut but not locked and this one was shut and very locked. I decided to break it with my Teolt.

“Hopefully this doesn’t set off any alarms.” I whispered to myself.

Luckily, no alarms went off. When I opened the door I found, for the most part, an empty room with a desk in the middle of the room and a chair. After gently closing the door, I walked around the room and noticed there were several paintings on the wall. One painting in particular stood out to me because it wasn’t straight like the rest of them. Walking up to it and correcting it, I can feel as if there was something behind the painting.

I lifted it up and found a hidden switch. My curiosity was too great and my impulsive thoughts took charge. Before I could think on whether to flip the switch, I found my finger on the switch already. The switch opened up a ground door disguised with floor boards. I felt this urge to go down the long staircase that led down the newly found opening. It was dark with a slight light blue glow at the very bottom.

I had a strange feeling about this, but if I was going to find my brother I'm going to have to take what felt like a risk. So here we go, now descending into the darkness towards the glow at the end of the staircase. As I got closer to the bottom, it started to feel cold. I began to embrace myself, my goosebumps were starting to come out on my skin. When I got to the bottom I was horrified by what I saw. There were at least 80 thick glass tanks. Each one had a glow and a person inside of it. Many of the people within the tank were in seriously bad shape.

I quickly wanted to help them, I saw all of them were connected to a machine that looked like a giant glass mirror screen. I slowly began to walk over towards the screen. Seeing a silver silk like moving swirl on it, I began to slow my pace even more. The closer I got, it began to show me glimpses of my past, and then present and then ...before it showed me what I knew would be the future next, I realized that the machines are powered by the Earth's prophets, and those who see the future. I quickly stepped away.

So this is how they are powering it, I thought to myself. Liriden has to be here. I looked around at all the big human thick glass tanks. Those who were still able to stand looked at me confused and disoriented. Their eyes were glowing a light blue glow. Just like the entrance when I got down here

"How am I going to find him in such a short time, people will notice I am missing and come looking for me. There's so many tanks." I thought aloud.

I noticed there were dates on the tanks and initials. These dates are dates within the past year, so it can't be birthdays. It has to be the dates they were taken. Liri was taken roughly when I started at Tlamatini. I began to look for that date and then initials. As I got closer to it I came across a girl that was beaten to a pulp. She was laying on the floor.

"Help.........m.."

She died shortly after. She wasn't moving anymore, and from the looks of it, she wasn't breathing either. I noticed her tank stopped glowing also,it's as if the life energy died so it couldn't power anything, like a battery. Scared for Liri's life, I looked around and noticed there were 10 tanks that were not powered. I need to move fast, I thought to myself again.

I continued to walk at a fast pace and all of sudden, a weak knock on a glass started. I looked at where it was coming from, and my face lit up with joy but my heart filled with the deepest sadness.

Guys....... I found him. I let Gio know.

Liriden was sitting on the floor with his head on the glass that divided him and I. He looked like he had been severely physically abused. He had whip marks on his legs still fresh, it seems like one of the lashes had cut too deep and he had open flesh. He had bruises everywhere on his arms and face. His eyes were glowing light blue like the rest of them and he had this broken smile, happy to see me. He wasn't as disoriented like the rest of them. Maybe it's because of his link with Lyla and Lumi. I quickly tried to get him out of there.

"How do I do this?" I asked. "I can break the glass." I told him as I gestured to him to step back.

He said no, because it would set off an alarm, it had to be done with a computer that was a few feet from him. He said and continued to say in sign language, that I had to put in a code. He has been watching them do it every time they brought someone in. His code was 7098, so I put it into the computer. All of a sudden one of his tank walls came down. But it wasn't the only one, two other tank doors opened but no one was in it.

"They knew, didn't they? They knew that there were two more. They just didn't get them that day." I asked Liriden.

He nodded softly and attempted to get up on his own, he fell right back down.
"Let me help you." I said as I walked towards him. All of a sudden a breach alarm went off. His

eyes widened in fear. He told me I had to leave, and to not forget him there. I wasn't going to forget because I wasn't leaving. I scooped him up the best I could, tossing his arm over my shoulder. He began to groan in pain.

"I know, I know, hang in there." I said as I put his arm over my shoulder.

And then a deep man's voice began to shout in the distance, " Hey! What are you doing here!"

Liriden was shaking his head, for me not to engage. I don't know what came over me, but seeing one of my little brothers in fear really triggered something in me.I felt this great anger in my chest, and my face was getting hot. I put Liriden to lean on one of the glass walls for a moment, he slid down into a sitting position on the floor. I stood up and stared at the man. I allowed myself to feel everything around me, the matter that everything was made of. Things were beginning to shake. Lifting the man up in the air I began to break every bone in his body, I combusted every vein in his arms and legs, I then squeezed his brain to mush. After all of this, I then dropped him to the floor.

My little brother looked at me in shock and a little in fear. In sign language, I told him he didn't have to fear me. I reached to pick him up once again, and it seemed like everything and everyone just loved to interrupt me because a sudden yank on my back sent me flying across the room. It was that Cohen guy, Richard Cohen.

After casually tossing me to the other side of the room he corrected his posture and fixed his sleeves by slightly pulling on the cuffs of his tux. I attempted to get up, my back was killing me. He did not go easy on me with that toss.

" I don't know who you think you are meddling in things you know nothing about, but you're about to meet your maker for doing so." He said.

" I already met my mom, thank you very much." I said sarcastically as I finally stood all the way up, very much in pain I dusted myself off and tried to straighten my now wrinkled dress the best I could.

" oh ...you're funny, huh?" He said as he began to make his way towards me.

But before I could even do anything to defend myself, suddenly , out of nowhere,

Richard got his jaw dislocated with a hit so hard it made a sound wave causing him to flip on his back. He was out cold.

When I realized who was now standing next to me, I smiled in relief. It was no other than the eldest of us, Evan.

"No one picks on, or hits my siblings but me, Mother Fucker." She said as she rotated her wrist and messaged her fist from the impact it had with Richards jaw.

At that moment I was so happy to see her. Lyla and Lumiere came from the direction of the staircase.

"Ohh, so it was you guys who breached the Manor." I said realizing my siblings probably did all the plans in one.

Lyla and Lumière ran to Liriden, they scooped him up and took him with them to the entrance of the staircase. I had a slight limp from the impact so I slowly walked towards the entrance also and Evan followed.

"Where's Gio?, I asked.

"He was the real breach", Lumière responded.

"What do you mean?" I asked.

"He broke through the main doors in his underwear." Lyla added.

"Yeah, he lost the bet with Lumiere so he had to do it. " Evan said, rolling her eyes as we made our way up the stairs.

" What bet?", I continued to ask.

" Gio had thought we weren't going to find Liri tonight, and Lumi said 'you want to bet' and they did." Lyla added.

"But we saw the bet happen four months ago in a vision of ours, we were interrupted that night so we didn't see a lot but the 'bet' conversation and Gio running in a building in his underwear." Lumiere said as he began to quietly laugh to himself.

They went out the window that Lumiere had burned a hole in by melting the glass, as we had originally planned. We gently lowered Liriden out the window.

" I have to go back to the Gala, it's still going. I don't want to tip anyone off." I said to all of them.

"That's fine, we'll see you at home, let Gio know we're clear." Evan said as she guided the triplets away.

"Will do." I said.

As I let Gio know, I casually made it to the washroom to make myself presentable. After getting my ass tossed across the room, I really needed to fix a few things, especially my hair. When I went back out I saw a picture on a side table of Professor Gregor and Leif.

"What the fuck?" I said, lifting the small frame up to look at it better.

They were straight faced in the photo, in what looked like fencing clothing. Putting the small frame down I began to shake my head gently, confused on the photo I thought to myself, "This doesn't make sense". I also thought this was a problem for another day.

Snapping out of it I snuck back into the Gala Hall where everyone was still enjoying the evening. It wasn't but 30 minutes later that the buzzing of conversations began to die down and people began to leave. I was surprised no one knew or heard the commotion that occurred down in the secret basement. I wonder if it was sound proof.

Leif and I left the event exactly at the time it was supposed to end. On our drive back to take me home, Leif stood mostly in silence. It was getting a little uncomfortable, so I began some small talk.

“Well I had a great time tonight.” I said as I thought about that toss across the room that he had no idea happened.

“I’m glad you enjoyed yourself.” He said as he focused on the road.

“I did! Those hors d'oeuvres really were something, I think that’s what kept me in the bathroom for a while.” I continued to say as I chuckled to myself.

He stood quiet.

“Is everything ok?” I finally asked.

This seems to be the question or conversation he really wanted to touch on.

"Sure, is everything ok with you?" He said a bit bothered.

"Are you ….mad at me?" I asked, confused.

"No! I can't be mad at you!" He started to raise his voice at me.

"What the fuck is wrong with you, Why are you raising your voice at me!" I began to raise my voice as well.

He shook his head, "Just forget it." He ended.

"I don't understand why you're so upset, Leif.", I said as I looked at him. He continued to look at the road while he was driving.

Pulling over on the curb of the road, he put the car in park. There was only about 15ish minutes left until we arrived at my house. He turned to me.

"You want to know why I am upset?" He asked, breathing heavily.

To be honest, I wasn't sure if I really wanted to know at this point. But I responded anyway, "Why?" I said softly.

Taking a deep breath in and slowly letting it out, "Remember how you asked me if I was Jealous of Alexander?" He said looking down and then at me.

"Who??.....Oh wait…you mean Professor Gregor? Oh yes, I remember.Why?" I asked.

"And I told you I wasn't." Leif continued.

"Yes?" I said.

"Well I lied. Truth is…… I am jealous. Of him… and every man that gets to be in your presence." He said looking deep into my eyes.

I, still in pain, trying to not show it, stood quiet to hear what he had to say

" I can't …. I just can't contain myself anymore, and this jealousy. When I see you with any other man…. It drives me insane, Reina. Because I want to be them, I want to be that close to you at all times. And tonight, when I saw you with

Alexander.... I can feel my blood boiling from seeing him, but a foot's distance from you, and when he kissed your hand.....the burning desire I had to have my lips on your skin like that ......" He stopped to give me a moment to react.

Lost of words, " I...I don't know what to say... but why are you upset at me?" I responded.

"I'm not, I'm upset with myself....for not thinking of it sooner......before he did." He said as he messed around with the steering wheel.

"And you're telling me this now?" I asked, a little confused. "Of all times we've spent together you chose now to tell me how you really feel?" I continued.

"I'm sorry but don't think I didn't notice your hair was slightly changed and your dress was wrinkled after Alexander left and you shortly after to *wash your hands*, unlike when we arrived." He said as he slowly trailed his eye from my knees to gradually meet my eyes.

"Are you.... insinuating ....what... I think you're insinuating?" I asked, bewildered by the audacity of this man.

He stood quite.

"You actually think I slept with Professor Gregor??" Anger began to slowly creep into my chest.

" I'm saying what I saw," Leif responded.

Upset with that response, " you know what, whether I did or didn't I suppose it really isn't your business..... at least not anymore." I got out of the car and slammed the door shut.

I left so upset and offended,I didn't realize how quickly I made it to the house. Unlocking the door and aggressively shutting it behind me, I made my way up the stairs to my room. Before going into my room I stopped by Mom's room and found mostly everyone surrounding Liriden ,who was now resting on Mom's bed. My anger faded away as I walked into her room.

Mom seemed to have fallen asleep on the chair that she has in her room next to her bed; Lumiere and Lyla were laying in Mom's bed with Liriden in between them both. All three of them were out like a light. They did not even notice I had entered the room.

Evan and Gio weren't in the room, they must be downstairs in the kitchen. I gently grabbed a throw that was at the foot of the bed and covered mom and left the room.

As I continued to make my way towards my room, I saw Sebastian in his room. I decided to make a stop there and give him a long overdue piece of my mind..

"Dude, what the fuck?" I said annoyed.

"Oh hey Reina." He said nonchalantly as he unpacked his bags.

"You were absolutely worthless in this mission to find Liriden." I said, still bothered.

“You know what Reina, I don’t need your negativity.” He responded as he took a folded shirt from his luggage.

“Do you even care about anyone other than yourself?” I asked. “You went to Italy to supposedly find someone in the ass crack of *BooFoo* land that you didn’t even know if they were alive or not.” I continued.

“It was a risk we took, yes, I know. But we went to find some answers in hope to find Liriden.” He responded.

“And did you? Did you find answers?” I asked, annoyed.

“Not entirely. But I did find a stone that mom might be able to benefit from.” He said as he continued to take things out of his luggage. He unzipped a side pocket of his duffle bag and pulled out a keychain with a knock off version of a Larimar stone.

I looked at him and scuffed, “Is this the stone for mom?” I asked as I took the keychain from him.

“Whatever Reina, at least I tried.” He said as he took it back from me.
“Your attempts are as strong as a toddler trying to keep its pacifier from an adult.” I said as I turned away to finally walk into my room.

Taking into consideration the sleeping heads in the house, I gently closed my door. But in all truthfulness, I wanted to slam the door so hard it would break the door frame. I began to get undressed. And as I took the dress off I can see the bruises on my body from being thrown across the room. Honestly, I'm surprised I survived that. A normal person would have ended up in the Emergency Room. I wonder if that's part of my ability? Or maybe I'm just built differently.

As my mind wandered from one thought to another, I began to think about what happened tonight and what I saw. And that photo of Leif and Professor Gregor. Why was there a photo of them in that Manor? Are they somehow related to all of it? Did they know? If only I had the answers.

Taking a deep breath in and then out, I decided to go for a bath. Gathering my clothes to head to the bathroom I noticed a note on my bed. I stopped in my tracks. It was a beige envelope with a red wax seal on it. I exhaustedly exhaled, as I stared at it. I did not want to open this new mystery envelope. I just wanted to shower and end the night with a nice bowl of cereal.Instead I decided to take a little time to grab the envelope from my bed. As I broke the seal and pulled out the letter within, I took a seat in my shower robe and read the letter. It was a letter from that IPWR company. It was a thank you letter for attending the event and that they look forward to seeing me soon,Signed by.... Richard Cohen.

An eerie sense came over me. More questions began to arise. One of which was "how did this letter get on my bed before I got home from the Gala?" I turned the letter over, it seemed there was more to see on the back.

I hope you enjoyed yourself Ms.DelaRosa, I will see you soon.

-R.C.

It then dawned on me that this man knows where I, specifically, live. Which made me feel unsettled. I was not comfortable with this information but most of all, I wasn't comfortable with the fact the letter was casually sitting on my bed. This made me feel as if he somehow had been here. I shook my head as if I was disagreeing with my thoughts. Placing the letter back on my bed, I realized I was still in my shower robe and needed to bathe. As I made my way into the bathroom, I put my towel, and folded pajamas down on the closed toilet. I turned the faucet on to let the hot water run. While the water ran, I took my flip flops off and stepped onto the soft rug. We had some floral bath bombs and epsom salt. At this moment I felt I needed all the *works*, so I poured both into the steaming bath water. Our bathroom had a shower and bath combination. So we had the best of both worlds. Tonight, I really needed to soak in a bath.

As I slowly submerged myself into the hot water, a knock came to the door. I was so tired of the day in general, I really didn't even want to answer. I just wanted to sit in my flower water and "cook" until my water turns cold. I ignored the knock and began to play with the water and the petals that floated about.

"The world could be falling apart right now, I don't care. Please leave me alone." I said calmly but clear enough so that whoever was knocking could hear.

They knocked a little harder.

Getting upset, I stood up from my bath and came out of the bathtub. Throwing my bathrobe on and tying it at the waist.

"Can't fucking catch a break", I said as I went and reached for the door. But before I could touch the door knob I felt a cold chill run down my back. I had this sudden feeling that there was something strange on the other side of the door but familiar. It was a familiar energy but I feared it to be almost like ... .death. I personally was not ready to see death just yet so, I slowly retrieved my arm and took a step back.

Another knock, and another, it was as if they were getting impatient.

All of a sudden; a silence, that was louder than the knocks, occurred. I no longer felt the intense presence anymore. I decided to grow some "lady balls" and open the door. Nothing and no one was there. I looked down the hall to see if anyone was down the hall or to see if anyone had heard or even reacted to the knocks. It seemed I was the only one who heard it. I wonder, was it all in my head? Did I imagine those knocks? I think I'm just freaking out, so I decided to finish up my bath and then shower to rinse myself.

After finally finishing my bath, I was all set back in my room. I saw Gio walk by my door.

"Gio, can you come in here really quick?" I hollered. He didn't come in, so I tried to communicate with him telepathically, but he didn't respond. Maybe he's tired, I thought and he doesn't want to be bothered.

I took a deep breath in and then exhaled. I began to feel tired myself, today was an exhausting day. I began to try to cuddle up with my covers and make my pillows comfortable. I slowly laid back, to rest my head on my pillow. I can feel my body going into a deep sleep.

“wake up..,...”

“wake up……..”

“Reina……..”

“You need to……”

“Wake…UP!!”

Chapter Twelve

"Wide Awake"

What started like a whisper began to yell at me.

“WAKE UP…..”

“WAKE UP ….”

“REINA!!……”

Breaking me from my sweet slumber , I woke up startled, looking around frantically breathing heavily. I checked the time on my phone that rested on my nightstand. It seems I slept, only a few hours. Was all that just a bad dream?

The ominous feeling of the yelling lingered. I tried to shake it off. But I couldn't.

Then, again.

“wake up…..”

I heard it again. I wonder if Gio is having a nightmare. And I'm just hearing his “telepathic sleep talk”?

Feeling concerned, I went to check on him in his room. His door was closed so naturally I knocked.

“Gio, hey gio. You good bro?” I asked as I tried to turn the door knob. But it wouldn't turn.

“What the fuck, Gio never locks his door.” I thought out loud.

“wake up…” again a whisper.

This whisper seemed familiar but I couldn't recognize it. It's as if every time I heard it, It became less and less familiar.

It was like the voice was telling me specifically to wake up. But the problem with that is, I was already awake.

“Wake up..”

"I am awake!!!" I yelled slightly annoyed from the repetitive demand

Making my way to my mom's room, I hollered toward her room if she's hearing a voice.

" A voice? No honey, I don't hear a voice. Do you hear a voice?" She responded.

"Don't answer …" the voice that's been telling me to wake up, whispered.

Confused and wondering why I shouldn't, but hearing the urgency in the familiar voice, it did not want me to tell my mom I heard it's voice.

" No, I was just wondering." I responded. "Hey, do you know if Gio's awake?" I added.

" Gio? He decided to step out for a second, he'll be back soon." my mom had hollered out of her room.

Something was off by her response. If he's out why is his door shut, closed and locked.

Why did it sound like she didn't know who Gio was? I went back to Gio's room and tried the door knob ,again. It wasn't budging. I didn't like any of it. I didn't like the fact that I'm hearing a voice telling me to wake up but I can't recognize it. I didn't like that my mom didn't seem to know who Gio was. I didn't like that this fucking door was locked. There was something about this door that was bugging me. I'm not sure if it's because it's locked or because I feel like there's something up. Like there is something behind it that I'm not supposed to see.

I felt like Gio didn't step out, I felt that he was in his room. And he needed me to wake him up, but it feels like I'm supposed to wake up.

Trying the door again, but this time I tried to use my Teotl.

"Wake up ..." it repeated.

"OKAY! I'm AWAKE!" I shouted back.

I began to focus on the door. It started to vibrate and the door handle began to shake back and forth. The door vibrations were caused by my Teotl. The door knob turning back and forth uncontrollably was not my doing. I tried to refocus my attention on opening the door.

All of a sudden mom was there,
"Uhm, what are you doing?" She asked.

I stopped and looked at her, " I need to open this door. Can you help me?" I asked her.

She looked at the door and then the knob, and back at me.

"Um, how about we go down stairs and drink some hot coco." She said while grabbing my hand to lead me toward the stairs.

" I'll be right down, I forgot I have to get something from my room." I responded calmly, taking my hand back.

She gave me a cold look, and then softened her face," okay, well don't take too long." She said as she headed down the stairs. Even her touch is off.

Listening for her footsteps to get into the kitchen, I quickly looked at the door, held onto the door knob and focused on this door.

This time, I didn't hold back.

The door vibrated aggressively. The wood of the door began to crack in multiple places. It looked as if it was starting to breathe with the cracks. And with the final concentration the door combusted into Gio's room. Except, there wasn't a room. There was darkness.

A pitch black void of darkness. And out of the darkness was a very small light. It looked like a single star in the night sky. And out of that light came a thunder of a voice.

"WAKE UP REINA" the familiar voice shot through the void and hit me so hard I felt it in my chest.

Mom came running up the stairs.
"What are you doing! Get away from there!" She shouted at me.

"WAKE UP!" The voice said again.

Looking back at mom, her face began to change. She was getting upset.

" Hey mom." I said.

“Yes?” She said upset.

“How come you didn't see this coming?” I said as I went into the void as the darkness closed up the door again shooting me towards the star like light. The closer I got the larger the light grew.

“Wake up” once more, the voice said.

And when I finally was close enough to the light, my eyes opened.

Chapter Thirteen

"The Wings"

I found myself tied up to a table, I was attached to a bunch of needles in my arms that were causing me pain. I looked around and saw Gio beaten and bleeding tied down to another table next to me. He was looking at me with a mouth piece covering his mouth. Evan was stuck in a red glowing cylindrical human size tube submerged under water with a mouthpiece also and needles in her arms. But they weren't the only ones, there were several other tables and red lit cylindrical human size tubes. Some empty, some filled. I looked around and noticed the triplets were missing.

Finally, getting my wits together. I looked at Gio. Through our telepathic connection, I asked about the triplets and what happened. He told me that we didn't make it out with our plan to save Liri.

“So it was you. The voice that kept telling me to wake up.” I said telepathically.

“ Yes.” He said.

“ Why do you sound different in my head?” I asked.

“It was some dude that works with that Richard guy. His ancestors worshiped the Greek god Hypnos. So I guess he inherited that Teotl.” He responded.

“ How do you know this?...... And so he messed with my brain?” I asked, looking around feeling a sense of fear and confusion.

“He was pretty cocky about his ability to do so, he said that I'd never get to you. But I think we fried his brain or something because Mr.Hypnos is on the floor over there bleeding from his nose and ears, unconscious. Even said he was going to make you forget my voice. I guess he did.” Gio said with a sad tone at the end.

“Not entirely, just keep talking to me. If we broke his hypnosis we can break that too.” I responded. “Now how to get out of here.” I thought aloud.

I tried to focus my energy on getting out and attempted to use my Teotl. But it seems I’ve been injected with some type of “IV” that affected my ability to use my Teotl.

“Reina, use your power to get us out.” Gio said telepathically.

“ I can't. I'm barely able to use our mind connection.” I responded out loud.

I thought and thought, how are we going to get out? I started to worry, I didn't want that psychopath, with the gifts from the Greek God Hypnos, to get up before we escaped. Frustration began to come over me. I began to move about like a wild animal that was tied down.

Gio’s eyes widened, “what are you doing, they'll hear you!” , he said telepathically.

“Well, what do you expect me to do!” I responded.

All of a sudden it sounded as if someone was coming.

Gio and I looked at each other, both with widened eyes.
"Play dead" I said telepathically while closing my eyes and head dropping.

"Well, I feel pretty close to dead right about now anyway, so." Gio responded jokingly as he closed his eyes.

The footsteps sounded as if they were getting closer, two sets of steps to be exact. I can feel a cold pair of hands touching my wrists. They were taking the bondages off of my arms, and the six needles that were injected into my arms, three on both arms. It hurt but I tried not to move, or give any notion of me being awake.

"Gio, I have a plan." I said telepathically.

"What's the plan?" He responded telepathically.

"You'll know in just a moment." I responded telepathically.

Waiting for the right moment, I listened.

“What happened to this guy?” A voice sounded sarcastic.

“Rory must have pushed himself too far. That idiot never knows when to quit. He’s practically addicted to messing with the minds of people.” Another voice responded.

“I wonder what he did to push himself so far that blood had to come out of his nose and ears?”

“ Ah, considering he’s between these two, he must have tried to juggle more than what he could handle. Which sucks, cause I really needed a Hypnos gifted person to move this one into a tube.”

I felt a slight tap on my foot. I guess I was the one they wanted to put in a tube like Evan was.

Ring ring

“Hello... yes, perfect. You have the package? Yes, we are almost done here, we’ll move the one girl into a tub for preservation and eliminate the other guy.... Yes, he’s not important. Well in case you forgot Richard, this is the Hybrid wing. All I have seen this kid do the past two months was flirt with his girlfriend and erase a few peoples minds. That's not really a duo ability. Do I need to remind you what we do in the hybrid wing? Yes, we put away all the Hybrids so that the prophecy of your family doesn't come true."

"Prophecy?" I thought telepathically.

"You think it's about that story we read about? The one with the oracle and the king." Gio responded telepathically.

"I am not sure, but let's listen." I responded telepathically.

"Okay, did he forget that his demise comes from 'two roots in one tree' or some bullshit like that? I mean that's what he said that those three little prophets said when he got close to them several years ago when he visited that school for his kid. What was it called again? Um, I think it was.....The school of....Tlamatini."

"That kid was a prodigy. Anyway, have you prepared that tub yet?"

"Oh shit, I completely forgot, my bad."

"Look, I know you're new here but if you mess up here anymore, it will most likely cost you your life. Understood?"

"Understood...... so, what now?"

"Well thanks to your fuck up, we need to let the tub prep for the next 30 minutes."

"So do we hook her back up, again?"

The voice sighed, "No, we can leave her like that. She should still be in the hypnosis state. Plus the fluids that have been running through her veins for the past few hours should have dulled her abilities."

"I guess you're right. Hey, it's pretty close to lunch, want to get some food while the tube prep?."

"That's probably the best idea you've ever had."

I can hear shuffling and the steps beginning to walk away.

"Hey, I never asked. What's in it for you? You're just a human."

"I'm in it for science. It's all very fascinating."

The voices began to turn faint along with the footsteps, while they kept conversing amongst themselves.

A few minutes had passed by. I wanted to make sure the coast was clear before moving a muscle.

"Gio....hey, Gio." I began to communicate telepathically.

A slight snore began to come out of him.
" You are not fucking sleeping right now." I said while opening my eyes to look at him. Beaten as he was, he opened one eye and smiled.

" I was getting bored with the conversation that Assistant Dingus and Dr. Science were having and not to mention having to play,'knocked out' actually allowed me to rest." Gio responded telepathically. "Anyway can you take this mouth cover off me since you're no longer tied down." He added.

"Right, let me get up." I said as I began to get up. As I lifted myself from the table, I felt a little lightheaded. I was not entirely stable, so I sat for a second to re-establish myself.

“Hey, you ok?” Gio said telepathically.

I nodded, and proceeded to get up to walk towards him. Taking off the mouthpiece that prevented him from talking, I then began to untie him from the table where he was lying.

Gio then got up. He looked dizzy.

“Are YOU okay?” I asked gio.

“Yes, I’m fine. In a bit of pain but fine.” Gio responded.

“Come on, we don’t have much time. We still have to get Evan and the others out.” I said while walking towards Evan, that was still floating in the human size tube.

Looking around and trying to figure out how to get her out without setting anything off. I noticed that there was a computer that was still signed in. On the computer screen I saw files with dates. One caught my attention, it was yesterday's date. Clicking into the folder there were 20 sub folders. I thought to myself, the dates must be the same as those containers that Liri was in. It seems that there are 20 more victims of whatever psychotic thing they are doing in this place.

Clicking into the folders I found that most of them had an image, a number code and a slight description of the abilities. But these focused on the severity of the powers that the person possessed along with their duo capability. I began to think there was definitely way more at work here. Finally, as I was looking through the files, I found a folder that had Evans face in it. It says that there's a potential second ability that is dormant. But the primary ability is *phenomena* speed. Gio eventually made his way towards where I stood.

" Did you find the code to get her out?" Gio asked.

"How do you know we need a code?" I asked.

" Well, it just makes sense, plus there's an "enter code" screen on that small tv that's attached to the tub she's currently in." He said, as he looked at me with a look of 'that was a no brainer'.

“You know what, I don’t need any of that negativity and judgment right now. I still have a bit of a foggy brain, you know.” I said as I turned back to the screen from looking at him. “Maybe this number is the code.” I added.

“It might be, it’s the only number that’s on her file.” Gio said as he made his way towards Evans human tube. “Welp, here goes nothing” he said before putting in the numbers.

I began to feel a tension build in my head from thinking so much about the potential alarms that might go off. I couldn’t help but scrunch my face, as if I was waiting for the whole tube to go boom.

*Beep Beep Beep ……Beep
Beep….Beeeeeeeeep*

Gio entered the last of the code.
My face still scrunched, I looked at him confused from that lack of explosion.
A second past and the tube began to make a strange sound. As if it was a giant plastic bottle with unopened soda in it.

Pssss

And then a "Gaglunk" right after. My face began to relax right after I realized the water that was in the tube began to go down along with Evan. She was no longer floating but coming to ground level. Once the water was all gone she was slumped at the bottom of the tube. Her arms had the same "IV" like injections in them. The glass that divided her from us went down.

"Come on, help me. We need to get that stuff to stop flowing in her veins." I said, quickly rushing to take it off. Accidentally removing the needles a little too rough, Evan was ripped from the sleep state she was in.

"Oww!" Evan yelled, snatching her arm away from me. "What's wrong with you! You couldn't be more careful?" She added.

"I'm sorry, but we don't really have time for the royalty treatment." I responded while trying to help her up.
She seemed a little unsteady, herself. But she was able to recuperate quicker than Gio and I did. It must be her immune system, working at the same speed she can run.

" I know where they have the triplets. I saw everything they were doing before they submerged me into the water." Evan said.

"Okay, where are they?" I asked.

"They're in another space, just out the double doors. I can show you guys." She responded.

"What about all of these other 'Hybrid' people? Shouldn't we help them escape too?" Gio asked.

"Unfortunately, there's not enough time for that. We need to get all of our siblings out to safety first. Granted, not Sebastien because his ass is probably on his honeymoon." I said, slightly disappointed, while gathering some tools I could use for defense, in case my Teotl didn't want to kick in when I need it too.

"There's one more thing." Evan said with a slight concern.

"What do you mean, 'there's one more thing'." I said as we began to quickly and quietly make our way to the double doors.

"They have mom." Evan said, looking at Gio and I.

This stopped me in my tracks. “I’m sorry, did you say ‘Mom’?” I asked still in disbelief.

“Yes, I saw them take her into the same space the triplets were.” She continued to say.

“Okay, okay, but why would they wan…” Gio started to ask out loud and then stopped. “Nevermind. I know why. She’s a visionary, one of the strongest one’s we know by the way.” He added.

“Stronger than the triplets?” I asked.

Gio and Evan looked at each other, then at me. “We’re not sure, actually. We’ve never seen the triplets use their abilities to the fullest. They’ve only played with it here and there for their shenanigans and mischief.” Evan said.

“I wonder if we will ever find out? “ I whispered as we approached the double doors to peek into the hall.

“Those double doors right across the hall. That’s where they are.” Evan said.

“Okay, Evan it seems your Teotl might kick in before Gio and I. I think it has to do with your metabolism or immune system. It works as fast as you run. Do you think you can check if the coast is clear in that space and come back, without getting caught?” I asked her.

“Remember guys, we only have 13 minutes left till Dingus and Science comes back.” Gio reminded us.

Evan began to try to use her Teotl. We can see her outer core slightly vibrating. She began to slowly nod. “Okay, I can do this, I’ll be back in two seconds.” She said,

It took less for her to flash away from our eye sights and one second for her to flash back. “It’s clear, we need to get in there fast.” Evan said.

“Okay, let's go.” Gio said.

As we crossed the hallway to go into the space ,we saw a label next to the double doors. It said, “ Visionary Wing”. We finally made it into the space they were in. It looked different then when we broke in, I thought to myself. I saw a familiar wall. I recalled the memory and the pain of the first incident, as I touched my back where the injury struck. The Visionary Wing seems to have more containers than the Hybrid wing. However, most of the containers were unlit. Some containers still have the essence of the previous victims. And, still there was a large population of visionaries.

We made our way through the rows of containers and found mom and the triplets. It was sickening to see that they would put a mom right in front of her kids. Allowing her to watch as they drain her and them from their life source for petty information they could just wait for, especially because that information is always changing, I felt anger creeping up on me. The Triplets were in containers all close to one another, like a triangle. Their eyes were all glowing the same as Liri, when we first found him. Mom's eyes were glowing too but her eyes were a white glow.

Hey ,Calm down. Don't lose your cool.

Gio said telepathically and looked at me.

"Let's just get them out." I said walking to the computer, trying to calm down.

I began to look into the folders they had. It seems they are really confident that nothing will go wrong in their system since they left all the computers unlocked. I was able to find their files. Liriden, Lumiere, and Lyla were all in one folder. They all have different codes but the same folder. I wonder if it's because they are a packaged deal. But it says they are only visionaries. I chuckled.

“That’s funny.” I said under my breath.

“What’s funny?” Evan said, cautiously looking around and walking over to the computer where I stood.

“It says the Triplets are only visionaries. That’s wrong, if only they knew they were….” , before finishing my sentence. We heard an alarm start to go off in the Hybrid Wing.

“Guys I think we’re out of time.” Gio said with a nervous tone.

“Quick pick a code and open the containers.” I said as I looked at one of the triplets code to put it in.

I opened Lumieres Container, he had a few bruises but not too roughed up. Evan opened Liridens and Lyla's, they were in similar states like Lumi. And Gio went to open mom's.

"Where the FUCK is your oldest brother." She said, with anger in her voice and her eyes were still glowing white.

"We don't know, we were out, ourselves. Last we knew about him he was in Italy." Gio Said.

"I'm going to have a word with him once we get home." She said, "Ese pendejo, va llevar, puñeta!." She continued.

We all looked at each other feeling a slight fear for Sebastien. We knew he was going to get his ass beat, no matter how old he is.

We were going to go through the double doors we had come through but two men came in through those same doors. It was Dr.Science and Assistant Dingus.

"You need to come back with us." The doctor said authoritatively.

"You're going to have to be a bit more specific Doc , there's several of us here." Lumiere said sarcastically with his eyes still glowing, slowly going back to normal.

Out of nowhere a quick swish passed by them sending them into the air.
"We don't have time for small talk." Evan said as she swiped her hands together.

"Okay, where's the original entry we came in through the very first time." I asked.

I think it's this way, Liri signed to us. *We made it as far as that room. Once we went out the window, there was one of those Hypnos dudes. That's what happened to you too , when you walked out the door to go back to the gala. It was another Hypnos guy waiting for you to leave.* Liri continued to tell us what happened as we began to walk towards the entry we came through in our first attempt to escape.

We began to see the blue lights like before. Quickly making our way up the stairs, we found ourselves at the top,slowly peeking our heads out into the room, somewhat reliving the experience. The difference however, this time around, the window that Lumi burned a hole in, had a wooden board on it. They must have boarded it up after we all got captured. Mom looked around and took the lead. It seemed like it was safe to come out completely into the room, so mom waved us to come out.

It felt odd, it's as if a strange sensation came over me.
"Mmmmm, I'm not liking this." I whispered as quietly as I could

.

"Me either but this is the way we know absolutely how to get out." Gio whispered back.

There was an eerie silence. We all slowly made our way towards the door of the room. Mom cracked the door open and looked to see if she saw anyone. It was quiet all around.

"Well this is suspicious. " Lumiere said.

"I have to use the bathroom."Lyla then said.

You're going to have to hold it like the rest of us. Liriden signed to her.

"We need to keep it down, where's the door to leave the building?" Mom asked us.

"It's about seven doors away after we turn right, passing the hall where the Gala was." I responded.

"Okay, has everyone fully recovered from that fluid that dulls our abilities, besides Evan." Gio whispered to us.

"Let me see." Lumiere said as he began to rub his thumb and index finger together. A small spark began to show until it turned into a small light.

"Okay, Lumi seems capable of using it. Let me try." Lyla started to try to manipulate the water that was in a clear vase on the desk in the room. She was able to move it slightly but couldn't completely manipulate the water. "It looks like I'm not 100 percent there." Lyla continued.

"Alright, well we have to move now or forever hold our peace." Lumiere said.

I don't think that's how that saying works. Liriden signed.

"Welp, it's how it works today." Lumiere responded while opening the door. "Let's go."

Chapter Fourteen

"The Truth"

We all cautiously spilled into the unlit hallway, and quietly made our way towards the main doors of the Manor. Our stealth skills were at its finest. However, when we began to approach the doors to the hall where the gala took place, we noticed it was slightly cracked open. The lights in the gala room shined out into the hallway where we were. We all stopped as if we almost stepped on a laser light that was going to set the place off in alarms. All of a sudden, we heard voices coming from the Gala room. Deep voices, it could have been at least two to three male voices, and then a woman's voice.

“If you weren’t so weak, we would not have to do any of this.” One of the male voices said.

“I’m not weak. If your head wasn’t so far up your ass, you would just love me for who I am. And not try to change me.”The second voice said. The second voice sounded familiar. “You’re always so focused on the money. Everything is money and power with you. I think you would even sell your soul to the devil if he granted you as much.” He continued.

A sudden smack sound came from the gala room. “Don’t you dare speak to me that way. You may be my son, but don’t forget who runs things here.” The first voice said.

“Sir, maybe there’s another way we can go about this.” The female voice said.

Does that person sound familiar to you? I telepathically asked Gio.
Absolutely, Gio responded.
That woman sounds like….

But before Gio could finish his sentence, a burnt smell all of a sudden began to come about.
“It smells like something is burning.” I said, as I turned to look back where we came from. It was not but a first glance looking in that direction and “poof”. I found myself having a hard time breathing and everything was so bright, close to

blinding. I wasn't the only one apparently. The triplets, Gio , Evan and mom were also gaspinging for air.

"Ah, Ms. DelaRosa. So kind of you to join us. And with none other than the family. Look, Sebastien, now you are all here." The male voice said.

My eyes began to adjust to the lighting in the room where we were now in. Looking around, I saw several familiar faces. One, I did not expect to see there at all was no other than my own brother, Sebastien. I felt confused, seeing him and then looking at everyone else. The first male voice we heard from the hallway was Richard Cohen, the Second was Alexander, and the woman was ….AzaRayah.

This feeling however, this lack of breath, the smell of smoke and the leftover smoke, I only know one person who can do that. Looking over my shoulder behind me, I saw Leif. Now I was really confused and began to feel betrayed on so many different levels.

Mom's eyes had adjusted to the light as well and when she saw Sebastien, she *blew up.*

"Qué carajo está pensando! Como tu puede hacer eto a la familia tuya!" She said as she went up to him.

"Wait mom, stop, I can explain…" Sebastien said before mom sent him into what I like to call, a *Vision Shock.* That's when mom would discipline us through her visions to keep us in line. She has not done that to us since we were kids.

Sebastien's body stiffened and he fell on the ground in a paralysis state. There was an awkward silence in the room for a brief moment.

"What did you do to him!?" AzaRayah said, reaching down for him.

"Ay por favor! Shut the fuck up, you hypocritical , conniving women. I should have listened to the ancestors and my Ex husband for that matter." Mom said as she walked away.

"What's going on? Why are you here Leif? And Professor Gregor, I mean Alexander?" I asked, part of me not wanting to know the answer I felt in my gut to be true.

Searching for Leifs eyes for the answer he had for me, and he avoided looking at me. I then looked at Alexander. He had a look of sorrow in his blue eyes.

“Well since you guys seem to be holding your tongue now all of a sudden. I’ll tell her.” Richard said, looking at the both of them and then at me.

“This here, in case you haven’t noticed, is my son, Alexander. He is one of four children. Unfortunately, my former wife and I lost one of our children so now there are three, But that’s not important right now. He was sent to work with the school and was tasked with sending me the list and files of the strongest students at the school, specifically the Hybrids. But he failed at doing that simple task, the way he does many other things. Ugh, he even failed to even be born with abilities. Pathetic.” Richard said as he pulled a chair from the seats that were already set from the Gala night.

“So you knew about all of this, the people , everything that was going on down stairs.” I asked Alexander, disappointed.

“Well hold on Ms. DelaRosa, I am not done telling you the whole thing.” Richard added.

"Leif was sent to spy on you, and bring me back intel on everything about you. You see I've been given this half assed fortune by several oracles. That I am going to die by one of two roots from one tree and that everything I had built including this empire would perish. Now, I wasn't sure if it was because that particular Oracle was upset about the one night stand I had with her , which at the time I didn't appreciate that comment much and well, Illuminated her. But I digress. It was a few years later when I went to visit my son, Alexander. I found these precious kids, no older than 13 years of age, I think it was?" He said looking at Alexander for approval of the time frame, which Alexander did not acknowledge him.

"Agh, anyway, these little kids were running about and one accidently bumped into me. I don't know what it was that triggered his vision but his eyes changed into a pale white glow. He started to talk. He told me things I never knew. Then the other two kids came looking for him and well, that's where I was inspired. Seeing all three of them in a form of trance. I realized these kids were not just any visionary that told the future. They told the Past, Present, and Future.." Richard paused for a moment.

I was listening but also thinking of ways to get out of here, Still uncertain if my abilities were going to be stable enough to fight back ,if need be.

"And well, I developed two businesses. One that allows me to see the future and even offer the knowledge of what is to come, at a price of course. Nothing is free in life. Even our necessities to live are something we need to pay,hmm. ... .And well the other was to find a way to fix my son while putting the Hybrids to bed. ...I'm not a bad guy" as he paused to get an approval from everyone around listening, " I mean come on. Give me a break. It was all in good faith."He would say sarcastically. "Use some of the abilities to put into my son, let him be normal for a change. It was a win, win. I wasn't trying to kill anyone." He ended.

"Don't even try to put all of those deaths in my name. I thought what we were doing was to help people! Not to mutilate them to get...what? A Possible chance of having an ability that the gods didn't give me. That would last a total of 5 minutes. And not to mention the process of getting it in me. It's a dangerous and serious process, even you have said so. Did you even stop to think that it might even kill me? Did you even think that you might lose your son." Alexander responded, in disbelief.

"I was willing to make the sacrifice if need be. I much rather have those options than to have you weak like your mother was before she betrayed me, with another. Now I really couldn't have that and a feeble child." Richard said as he stood up from the seat he had sat in.

"I hate you." Alexander said, with a heartbreak in his voice, as a tear escaped one of his eyes.

Richard scuffed at Alexander,"Well you can't pick your family, right? I mean I wouldn't have picked you.

"Well this has been great and all, I think you two have a lot to discuss, we will be heading out." Lumiere said, trying to gather everyone in our family to go towards the door.

"Not so fast, DelaRosa's" Richard said as he waved his hand causing the doors we were trying to leave through to shut abruptly, telekinetically. "I don't believe in killing people but I love making room for exceptions. Besides, you guys know way too much just for me to let you go." He said with a malicious smile.

Looking at each other we all slowly turned around to face them again.

"Dad, please just let them go. Haven't you done enough?" Alexander said.

"Ohhh, but we can never have enough." Richard said as he cracked the tensions of his neck and then shook his head.

"Well, I guess there's a first time for everything." Lyla said.

"What do you mean?" I asked.

"Family Power!" Lumiere said, while shimming.

Richard Laughed, "Please you guys don't stand a chance."

"Reina, I'm sorry." Alexander said.

"Well let's not just stand here. It is a Ball room after all, let's dance." And with that Richard made the first move. Trying to strike Evan. But she was too fast for him. We all began to move to fight Richard. Evan was able to land a strike on him. Gio went to get close to mind melt him but wasn't successful, He got tossed across the room, being left unconscious.

I went to charge at him, but before I could even do so I found Leif holding onto my arm, preventing me from moving forward. " Let go of me, Leif!" I yelled in frustration and bewilderment at the fact that he was trying to stop me.

"I can't let you do this." He said.

"What exactly? DO WHAT!?" I asked, still thinking of the audacity this man has.

"I can't let you get yourself killed. You are not strong enough to take this guy on." Leif said while trying to pull me towards him.

"Well, it's a little too late for that now, isn't it?" I said looking straight into his eyes. I then yanked my arm away from him and turned back to the chaos that was now going on.

I suddenly saw the triplets begin to start to move around as if they were doing ballet, this caused literal confusion to Richard and Everyone else. I thought to myself, my family has officially gone mad. But it was the type of madness that gave us enough time of distraction to plant another hit on Richard.This was making him upset. Then, these smoke-like tentacles began to come from the shadows of things in the room. One of the tentacles grabbed hold of Lyla, dragging her toward the dark corners.

Lyla began to scream. It took seconds before Lumiere and Liriden had dropped to the floor as well and began to scream too.

"AHHHHHHH, it burns!" They all started to yell together.
Lumiere was able to create a light bright enough to make the shadow tentacle release Lyla.

Covering my eyes enough to not be fully blinded. I tried to focus my energy to use my ability, it was as if my Teolt wanted to come out but it was still recovering.

"Lumi! I can't see! Tone it down!" I said while continuing to charge towards Richard.

Evan was zooming around, landing hits on Richard, until he created a smoke around him to blur her vision. Catching her off guard he was able to manipulate the air within the smoke around him and tossed her across the Ball room.

“Evan!” I shouted in shock.

And in that moment, it seemed mom had enough of it all. She pushed AzaRayah , who was standing by as if she was waiting for instructions, out of the way.

Mom stormed up to Richard, breaking through his mystical smoke. He seemed to have been caught off guard and looked startled, when she reached to grab his face with her both hands.

“You want to see the future? You want to know what is coming? Well here you go!” She shouted at him as she began to channel energies from all directions. I have never seen her use her Teotl this way before.

The Manor began to shake the way the house did that one day. There were two chandeliers on the roof that began to shake and sway as if the Manor was a ship on water. I began to feel that ground rumble from beneath my feet. She began to float in the air with Richard still in her grasp. Her eyes glowed pale white.

"AHHHHHHHHHhh, STOP! LET GO OF ME!" Richard Began to shout as he tried to break loose of my mothers grasp.

"Baracutey.....Bana........Bara!" Mom started to speak in what seemed to be tongues, again. But this time it was different. She then began to speak English with several different voices with her everytime she would speak. As if they were echoes of the past,
"Solitary....Greatness......Death..." She continued to say.

"YOU WILL FALL THE WAY YOU HAVE RISEN.... and in your own empire." Mom said with a strange smile. "You were so afraid of death, and greedy for all sorts of power, that you never even realized who you had right next to you. " She continued to say and then looked over to Alexander.

"You poor thing. If he only knew the greatness you will do in the years to come. And your own power you have." Mom looked back at Richard. "And you will never be there to see it happen, you will perish to ash. No one will remember you, no one to think of you, no one to even know of your absolute existence." She ended with a haunting smile as she continued to burn his brain with information and details of his future.

"NOOOOO, AHHHHHH.....You will pay for this you crazy bitch!" Richard shouted as he saw everything that mom continued to show him; several flashes of his future at once, or at least it seemed like it. The way his eyes moved left and right, in a rapid speed they began to start to tear in blood.

"Bitches" Mom sassed in the most expressionless face she had ever given as her voice began to echo with multiple voices. Richard looked at her confused and disturbed.

"If you are going to do an insult ... .Make sure to address everyone you are talking to. I mean .....you are .....speaking to...... everyone in this bloodline, including the Generations of centuries and centuries ago, so far back as the Taino Tribe." Mom ended.

This made Richard Cohan feel uneasy.

And it was at that moment, he gave the signal that AzaRayah appeared to have been waiting for. As soon as she saw the signal, she reached into her pocket and pulled out what looked to be a small remote. AzaRayah had seemed to call in reinforcements of some kind. They were more so, a form of distraction. It was like extra work. We all took on one of Richards goones, fighting a fight that seemed endless. There was a sense of hope as we fought back. It was as if we began to triumph. It was not till more men charged in out of nowhere that ripped mom out of her trance and in that split second the world stopped and so did all of our hearts.

Chapter Fifteen

"Rage is Red, Hearts are Blue"

Catching everyone off guard, a large spike like tentacle solidified and went straight through moms back and out of moms chest, knocking the air out of her. When the spike withdrew her back pulling blood out with it, mom dropped to the floor from floating five feet in the air, along with Richard. He then backed away from her and stood up holding his head. Trying to straighten himself out.

He began to smile and laugh nervously. He looked at all of us and then to me and pointed while he smiled mischievously. “You did this, Ms.DelaRosa. It was all you.” He said as he began to straighten his posture.

“ Nononononono.” I began to say as I ran to my mom that stood motionless on the floor. Mom,

mom, nonono…NOOOOOOO! Mom! No, please,Mom, you can't leave, you can't leave me. Mom!" I held her close trying to find a way to stop the bleeding. "Mom, hang in there. Please, don't leave me here , not alone. How am I supposed to do this without you!! Please…." I began to whimper. I can feel the warm tears escaping my eyes. I held her closer to me in my arms. She looked at me for a split second and I felt her slowly letting go. I couldn't help but wail out the agony of losing my mom. I sat there in a kneeling position,with her lifeless body. Just rocking her back and forth.

"You see, all that you have caused Ms.DelaRosa? No one needed to die." Richard said sarcastically.

I slowly and gently laid her on the ground and stared at her. My tears were still flowing. All of a sudden from one second to the next. I found myself shifting from my crying to a manic laughter. My blue heart still felt as if it were in the pit of my stomach but for some reason I couldn't stop laughing. My tears continued to pour out of my eyes.

I managed to put together a sentence through the breathing breaks of my manic laughter.

"AHAHAHAHhahaHAh, I'm going to fucking HahahahHAH kill you. HAHAHAHA Erase you from this earth, HAhAHHA until there's nothing but dust! HAHAHAHAHHha, there will be nothing left of this so-called empire." I said as my Teotl broke loose from the hold that injected fluid had on it.

I can feel everything, the ground, the construction of the building, the people around me, the people below us. Every container we saw, and last but not least Richard Cohan. Everything began to shake. The windows in the Ballroom combusted.

"Reina!" The triplets began to call for me.
I felt my feet leave the ground. My focus was directly on Richard Cohen. I can hear my name being called by my siblings but it was all so faint. It was as if it was being drowned out by the rage and pain I now carried in my chest. I can feel the walls begin to crack around us.

And at that moment, I allowed myself to be the villain of his story.

I mean ....after all ...... It runs in my blood.

www.ingramcontent.com/pod-product-compliance
Lightning Source LLC
Chambersburg PA
CBHW030607310726
48979CB00003B/608
* 9 7 9 8 9 9 0 3 5 5 2 0 0 *